PENGUIN

THE ANNIHILATOR

RuNyx is a *New York Times*, *USA Today* and international bestselling author of romance. Her stories range across subgenres from dark contemporary to gothic to historical to fantasy and more, and are currently being translated into over 10 languages.

Her pen name has a very special meaning to her. When she's not writing, she's reading, traveling, meditating, daydreaming, and most of all, procrastinating.

THE ANNIHILATOR

RuNyx

PENGUIN BOOKS

PENGUIN BOOKS

UK | USA | Canada | Ireland | Australia
India | New Zealand | South Africa

Penguin Books is part of the Penguin Random House group of companies
whose addresses can be found at global.penguinrandomhouse.com

Penguin Random House UK,
One Embassy Gardens, 8 Viaduct Gardens, London SW11 7BW

penguin.co.uk
global.penguinrandomhouse.com

Published in Penguin Books 2025
001

Set in 9.92/14.06pt Adobe Caslon Pro
Typeset by Six Red Marbles UK, Thetford, Norfolk

Printed and bound in Great Britain by Clays Ltd, Elcograf S.p.A.

The authorised representative in the EEA is Penguin Random House Ireland,
Morrison Chambers, 32 Nassau Street, Dublin D02 YH68

A CIP catalogue record for this book is available from the British Library

ISBN: 978–1–911–74636–2

Penguin Random House is committed to a sustainable future
for our business, our readers and our planet. This book is
made from Forest Stewardship Council® certified paper.

To everyone who cannot find themselves in a world full of people.
Being lost is a hard prologue, but a much beautiful story awaits you.
Find the courage, and turn the page.

Author's Note

This is the fifth book in the *Dark Verse* series. Although the book deals with a new couple, there are characters and events from the previous books that heavily influence the plot in this. Reading the series in order ***(The Predator, The Reaper, The Emperor, The Finisher***, in that order) is recommended for the best reading experience. This is **NOT** a standalone.

Please note that this book ends on a semi-cliffhanger, and the entire series will be wrapped up in the final book coming in 2022. More on that at the end.

If you have read the previous books, this one is the darkest of them. Truly, heed these trigger warnings. Being inside the head of these characters is a truly dark place to be in—one is borderline sociopathic/psychopathic and the other is intensely traumatized. This book includes graphic violence, foul language, and sexual content recommended only for 18+. Like *a lot* of sexual content. This might be the book I've written with most sex scenes. Sexual trauma is a part of this story, and so sex is also used in healing, and it works between these characters for development and growth.

Content warnings: This book contains scenes of light somnophilia, light breath play, light knife play, voyeurism, power play, light spanking, consensual non-consent, psychopathic behavior, stalking, blood, human trafficking, sexual slavery, sexual assault on a minor, child abuse, skin trade, murder, arson, assassination, torture, rape, forced drug abuse, mentions of organ trade, mentions of suicide, suicide ideation, depressive episodes, post-traumatic stress disorder, Stockholm syndrome, BDSM.

If reading about any of these is in any way detrimental to your mental health, I sincerely urge you to pause.

If you continue with the book, I hope you enjoy the journey.

Thank you.

Book Playlist

Terrible Thing - *AG*
Play With Fire - *Sam Tinnesz ft. Yatch Money*
Gangsta - *Kehlani*
Guest Room - *Echos*
In Flames - *Digital Daggers*
I Want To - *Rosenfeld*
Devil's Backbone - *The Civil Wars*
Devil's Girl - *Overnight ft. Melody Michalski*
The Wolf in your Darkest Room - *Matthew Mayfield*
Dark In My Imagination - *Of Verona*
Light a Fire - *Rachel Taylor*
NFWMB - *Hozier*
Live Like Legends - *Ruelle*
Can't Help Falling in Love (Dark Version) - *Tommee Profitt ft. Brooke*
Heavy In Your Arms - *Florence and The Machine*
Arms - *Christina Perri*
Like Lovers Do - *Hey Violet*
Like U - *Rosenfeld*
Horns - *Bryce Fox*
Jekyll & Hyde - *Bishop Briggs*
Heaven - *Julia Michaels*

Not Your Baby - *Cadmium*

Rabbit Hole - *Aviva*

Play Dirty - *Kevin McAllister ft. Sebell*

Do It For Me - *Rosenfeld*

Castle of Glass (Acapella) - *Linkin Park*

Dark Nigths - *Dorothy*

Sanctified - *Nine Inch Nails*

Caught in the Fire - *Klergy*

Us vs. Them - *Denmark + Winter*

The Devil Within - *Digital Daggers*

Secret - *Denmark + Winter*

Mind Games - *Sickick*

Castle - *Halsey*

Vacant - *Echos*

Walk On Fire - *RAIGN*

Heavenly - *Cigarettes After Sex*

Let Me Out - *Hidden Citizens*

Darkside - *Oshins feat. HAEL*

25 - *The Pretty Reckless*

Pyrokinesis - *7Chariot*

Toxic - *2WEI*

Love and War - *Fleurie*

Heart Heart Head - *Meg Myers*

Daddy Issues - *The Neighbourhood*

I Wanna Be Your Slave - *Måneskin*

Dark Side - *Ramsey*

Fetish - *Selena Gomez*

OMG - *Marian Hill*

Blood + Water - *Grandson*

Saints - *Echos*

Trouble (Stripped) - *Halsey*

Fire of Love - *Jesse Jo Stark*
Cherry - *Lana Del Rey*
Fallin' - *Sufle Ft. Gökcan Sanlıman*
How Villains Are Made - *Madalen Duke*
Sick Thoughts - *Lewis Blissett*
Unholy - *Hey Violet*
Hurt Me Harder - *ZOLITA*
Middle of the Night - *Elley Duhé*
Battle Cry - *Imagine Dragons*
Arsonist's Lullabye - *Hozier*
Blood on Your Hands - *Veda*
Animal - *AG x MOONZz*
The Devil is a Gentleman - *Merci Raines*
Madness - *Tribal Blood*
Love into a Weapon - *Madalen Duke*
The Death of Peace of Mind - *Bad Omens*
I'm Losing Control - *X-Ray Dog*
Serial Killer - *Moncrieff x Judge*
See You Bleed - *Ramsey*
Real Boy - *Lola Blanc*
Flames - *Tedy*
Massacre - *Kim Petras*
Paint It Black - *Hidden Citizens*
Slave - *Ramsey*
One Way or Another - *Until the Ribbon Breaks*
Nothing's Gonna Hurt You Baby - *Cigarettes After Sex*
Lost in the Fire - *The Weeknd ft. Gesaffelstein*
This is War - *Thirty Seconds to Mars*
There's a Hero in You - *Tommee Profitt ft. Fleurie*
Forever - *Labrinth*
Every Breath You Take - *Chase Holfelder*

Reflections - *The Neighbourhood*
Not Afraid Anymore - *Halsey cover by Roniit*
I Wanna Be Yours - *Arctic Monkeys*

THE MOON

Alone.

Silent.

Locked in.

Hands around her knees.

Shivers wracked her slight frame.

Locks of hair hanging limp over her shoulders.

She took a deep breath in, resisting the urge to look around herself.

She'd been shoved in the little closet for hours, each hour becoming more and more unbearable.

The dark, which had been oppressing her little mind, gradually became familiar. The blackness that had been a stranger, now a new friend, enfolding her in its arms.

Her own arms relaxed as her legs folded, crisscrossing on the cold ground, and her fingers started playing.

Playing with the locks of her hair, over and over, again and again.

To see, she stopped trying to blink.
She just breathed easy now.
Three was her age.
Locked in.
Silent.
Alone.

THE SHADOW

Fire.

Heat, warmth, and light.

Heat, destruction, and death.

The nature of fire had always fascinated him, the colors even more so. He liked watching the blue flickering in the heart of a blaze, turning into a yellow so white it could blind a man, deepening into oranges and reds like the sun setting over the sky.

Yeah, he liked fire. He always had.

He remembered the first time he had become fascinated by the flames. A boy in the orphanage with him constantly complained about burning under his skin all the time. The idea of it had fascinated him. Then he had seen the flames, colors searing into his vision. The rest of the world, the rest of the colors, never appeared quite right to him. The caretaker of the orphanage had said it was because he had demon eyes, because he was a demon child. He had named him after death too.

Maybe he was, because that very week he had set the man alight and smiled as the sparks danced over his body, the sound of his screams the only irritant in the picture. He didn't like it when they screamed. The noise fell sharply on his ears, tasted sour on his tongue. He didn't understand why he could taste sounds, but it wasn't pleasant with the screams. No, he rather enjoyed they be quiet while he came out of nowhere, the split-second look of something visceral on their faces before he mastered their death.

He hadn't always understood what that look had been. Emotions escaped him. He saw them, and could recognize them afterward, but he didn't understand what that terror felt like, or how the pain was experience. How others laughed and cried and empathized and he felt nothing.

Perhaps that was why she caught his attention.

Maybe it was because she emoted more than he had ever seen anyone emote. Maybe it was the flame in her hair. Or maybe it was because she had bound them with something she couldn't take back.

Whatever it was, from the moment her fire had found his, her fate was sealed.

He sat in the shadows watching her.

The strobing lights in the auction club went over the stage, three women in translucent robes standing in the center. He didn't look at the ones on the sides, his heterochromatic eyes on the one in the middle. He studied her, the way she blinked at her feet, her face dead to the world. The only sign of her life remained her hair, hair that had grabbed his attention since that first time.

He pretended to sip on his drink, wondering who there was going to die by his hands tonight. They all knew never to bid on her, a trail of bodies of her suitors sending a loud message. Yet, someone always did. Someone always tempted their fates. And someone always died. Last time, it had been a sniper bullet through the brain, the poor shit's blood splattering across her pale skin. This time, he'd make it more personal. Maybe douse them in gasoline while she watched.

As though feeling his gaze, she looked up. Her eyes swept the crowd of well-dressed men, going straight to the shadowed corners, knowing that's where he stayed. He liked that.

He saw the moment she saw his silhouette, a mix of hatred and betrayal etched on her face for everyone to see. Her hands fisted at her sides. His obsession deepened.

Though she wasn't a blaze yet, only an ember, she was his.

He watched her, intently focused on the nuances of her face.

One day, she would be an inferno, and he would be the devil who controlled it.

PART 1

ASHES

"Into this wild abyss, the wary fiend stood on the brink of Hell and looked a while."

—John Milton, *Paradise Lost*

CHAPTER 1

LYLA, 5 YEARS AGO

It was her first time in a sex club. Though she had heard about them, she knew many girls who were taken into them, she had somehow never found herself there.

And *Moonflame* was as upscale as it could get. Her buyer for the night, a gray-haired man with an expensive watch and a nice suit, held her waist as he led her down the corridor and into the wide open hall. It was dripping with luxury, from the chandeliers on the high ceilings to the velvety red couches to the gleaming wood. It was luxury she glimpsed in her darkest moments, only to return to nothingness.

Lyla watched people in various stages of undress sitting around the lounge areas, simply talking and sipping their drinks, some men and women wearing masks while some of the girls and boys remained bare-faced. It was a party for those who could afford it, and Lyla could feel the power pushing at her from all sides.

Swallowing down her nerves, unprepared, she followed the man as he guided her to a door at the other end of the luxurious hall. He had been a smart one—he hadn't bid on her at the auction. Instead, he'd come straight to the complex she lived at and purchased her for a year, and Lyla was terrified because she didn't like the sadistic look in his eyes, and she didn't know if *he* even knew about her new contract. *He* usually just watched the auctions, so she didn't know how he could know of a deal that went through during the day.

Dressed in a black gauzy chiffon dress that tied at her waist, without any underwear, she dreaded what was to come of the night as the gray-haired man led her into an auditorium of some kind. There was a stadium-like arena with couches on elevated levels at her back, people on them watching. But instead of an empty middle area, there were tall red walls lining it up, only one opening in the middle for entrance.

It was a maze.

Before she could even grasp the full sight, the monster at her side turned her to the audience, tugging her dress open so her breasts popped out to their lecherous gazes.

"Ladies and gentlemen," he announced. "Whoever catches my slave tonight gets a chance to play with her."

Horror ripped into her, her eyes flying over the masked and unmasked people. They were sick. Every single one of them. So sick.

"No." The word escaped her before she could control it, and she felt a large hand strike her cheek.

"You don't speak, girl!"

Skin burning, she looked down at his feet, her brain warring with anger and pain and disgust, knowing she was helpless to stop this. The monster pulled her hands tightly behind her back, tying her wrists up with some kind of rope that abraded her skin.

"Run," the monster slapped her burning cheek lightly. "Save yourself for a few minutes before we find you."

Adrenaline filling her veins, she didn't wait a moment before darting into the maze, escaping the eyes on everyone. The walls closed in around her, a head higher than she was, enough to keep her hidden from the watching eyes. She took a deep breath, looking both ways, before darting to her right and running full speed until she came to a dead end. Chest heaving, half her dress undone, she pivoted to the left, with no clue where she was going, just wanting to run and escape, but the powerlessness of knowing there was no escape made her eyes burn.

She hated them.

She hated every single one of them for making her feel inhuman.

The tears stung her burning cheek, going down her jaw and falling, as she turned and ran.

She heard the laughter around her, heard some of the voices closer than they should have been, and the walls closed in on her even more. She couldn't even stop and hide herself, knowing they could see her from their seats above, and god she wanted to kill them all, completely destroy them for treating her like this. She'd done nothing to deserve this. *Nothing.*

After a minute or an hour, she didn't know, she turned left and came to a stop, looking at a little opening in the middle of the maze. From where she stood, she could see around the entire auditorium, and she realized she was in the dead center, in the visibility of others. There were five men on the couches above, one of them getting his dick sucked by a girl, two of them fucking a girl, the other two jerking each other off. A masked woman sat on another side, watching the scene and getting eaten out by a girl.

So many people watching her be helpless, and none of them willing to find a shred of humanity to help.

Two men emerged from the other end of the maze, their masks keeping their faces hidden, and she braced herself as they came toward her.

Heart in her throat, she watched as they grabbed her arms and dragged her to the middle of the room even as she struggled to get away, her struggles futile. Seconds passed, the men talking to each other in a foreign language, their hands tight on her biceps.

Defeated, she closed her eyes, and prepared herself to lose.

And suddenly she heard it.

Gasps and screams rang out in the air, and she opened her eyes, blinking, unable to understand why everyone who'd been watching seemed to be rushing out.

Her buyer, the gray-haired monster, sat on a couch, his throat slit open, red drenching his white shirt. Lyla watched, aghast, as the others ran out from an exit just as a blade flew and embedded itself into the neck of one of the men holding her. Something warm splattering on her breasts, the grip on her arms loosening, Lyla looked down at the blood on her body in shock. The other man holding her left and began to run, only to have a blade embedded in his back.

Terrified, filled with a deep-rooted instinct for survival, she jumped back into the maze, and pressed herself into the wall, running toward relative safety. Whoever had issues with her buyer, she didn't want any part of it. Knowing she was visible from the elevated ground, she somehow managed to crouch and run, making herself as small as possible, her breaths heavy as her arms strained behind her back in the restraints.

Finding a corner away from the direct line of sight of the seating area, she straightened, catching her breath, her eyes wildly scanning for any danger.

And she felt a blade touch the nape of her neck.

Stilling, her body fraught with tension and her heart fraught with fear, she froze.

The blade traveled down the line of her spine, the sharp point just on the surface of the skin. A little pressure and it would rip her open. She closed her eyes, the sensation inducing fear and something else inside her, hoping against hope the killer didn't torture her.

She felt a warm, tall body press into her front as the blade kept traveling over her back, and she clenched her eyes shut, her arms shaking.

A breath on the side of her neck, the scent of something familiar in her nose, and the voice of death in her ear.

"Eyes, flamma."

Her eyes flew open, shock, something else filling her system as she tilted her head back.

Devilish, mismatched eyes locked with hers through a mask, and her breath caught.

He'd come.

He'd come for her.

He'd killed for her.

Lyla began to sob, intense, acute relief flooding her body.

As his blade ripped through the restraints holding her wrists, she launched herself into his chest, feeling his body freeze and she clung to him, her tears wetting his shirt, his scent ensconcing her, his warmth chasing the chill from her bones.

She felt one of his hands hold her wrists behind her—similar to the restraints but somehow she didn't feel bound—the other hand coming to grip her jaw. His thumb traced her lips before tracking the tears on her cheek, his gaze watching her cry in something akin to fascination.

His lips came to her cheek, his tongue darting out to lick her tears, before he pulled back, watching her with such innate possession she felt it in her marrows.

"I didn't think you'd come," she whispered in the space between their lips, her body overcome with the emotions she'd felt in the last few minutes.

His gaze intensified, and he leaned down, speaking right against her mouth, his words brushing her lips but barely, *so close* she felt them on her skin, a promise and the threat all in one sentence both claiming and capturing her.

"I'll always come for you."

CHAPTER 2

LYLA PRESENT DAY

The monster was going to die.

She sighed inwardly, watching the middle-aged man old enough to be her father walking toward her in the auction room after winning his bid. The dark ambiance amplified by the strobes of light didn't hide either his good looks or his dripping wealth. Well, he had to be wealthy to get a foot in the auction door, and his looks didn't mean a thing. She'd been with worse. More importantly, she knew better than most how the worst monsters lurked beneath a pretty face. They came below to this hellhole to live out their most detestable fantasies, ripped and shredded and went back to their facades above of being upstanding, moral citizens with wives and families and picket fences. She hated those kind the most. It was easier to deal with a monster who was a monster upfront and not a snake in the grass.

The man's eyes took in her form on display in the translucent robe, going from her neck down her ample breasts down to her waxed mound down to her painted toes, and even after so many times, she barely controlled her flinch at the lecherous perusal.

She knew why they bid on her. She was a rarity, an exotic natural redheaded delight in a sea of blondes and brunettes, and she was attractive. She brought in good fucking money at every bid, which was exactly why the organizers kept putting her up on the stage and the idiots kept risking their lives. They all thought they'd be the one to get away with it, blinded by their power and arrogance.

They were wrong. For six years, they had been wrong, every single one of them, and there were over a dozen corpses to speak for it.

Before she could fall into her thoughts, she schooled her expression to the one of serene calmness that her early handlers had taught her.

"You are soft, inviting. Look pretty, lower your chin, and stay silent."

The man—she was calling him Fifteen in her head since he was the fifteenth man to buy her at the auction—stepped close to her, taking a lock of her long, wavy hair in his hands.

Oh, he shouldn't have touched the hair.

She didn't voice the thought.

"What's your name, sweetheart?" he asked with a smooth grin, the lasciviousness in his eyes naked enough for her to know exactly what he was thinking.

"Lyla," she spoke quietly, exactly at the volume she had been trained to talk at.

Every girl got trained in a way that suited their looks to make them seem most appealing. For Lyla, everything was supposed to be soft, docile, meek—her voice, her mannerisms, her demeanor. She had to give off sexy siren and sweet submissive vibes all at once.

One of her only friends, Malini, had been trained exactly in the opposite way. She was bold and forward. She'd been told to behave wildly, to make a man want to tame her. A small sliver of amusement spiraled through her at the thought. The trainers had it all wrong. It was all an act they did. Malini was the gentlest, sweetest soul. Lyla could not remember the number of times she had sought out her care when the other girl had soothed her in ways she imagined mothers or sisters soothed their loved ones—with light touches and soft words and enough love to make her want to see another day. But she hadn't seen her friend in a few months, and when she'd asked around, one of the handlers told her a man had taken her for a long contract. That could mean years before she saw her again, if she ever saw her at all.

"And how old are you?" The buyer's words broke through her thoughts, making her focus again. She knew exactly what men like him wanted, and even though she was twenty-four, she said, "Eighteen."

The man smiled. *Fucking asshole.* Although he at least tried to cloak his monstrosity, she had seen too many adults rip through innocence to believe in decency anymore.

The man touched her breast unabashedly and she stayed still, her hands fisting at her sides as she let him test the weight of them.

He wasn't just going to die, he was going to *die.*

She held her breath, her eyes roving over the dark corners of the room, unable to see the silhouette of the devil in the shadows, one who was both the bane and the blessing of her cursed existence. As the hand pawed her, she let her mind drift to the first time she'd seen *him* at the auction six years ago, the second time she had seen him ever. She remembered the surprise she'd felt, mainly because she hadn't thought she would find him again, and she'd felt hope that he would bid on her. She had wanted him to be the one to choose her. He hadn't. He'd stayed in his corner and simply watched as another man won her and took her to the hotel a block away from the auction house.

That had been the first night she'd felt the spray of blood on her face, a bullet-hole gaping through the head of the man who'd been about to undress her. She had frozen on the spot, her eyes going out the window to the silhouette of a man moving in the building opposite, and she had known it was *him.*

Lyla watched the shadowed corners as Fifteen in the present leaned down to kiss the side of her neck while tugging at her breasts openly in auction room. The corners were empty but that meant nothing. She knew better now.

He was watching. He was *always* watching.

She'd learned that the second time she'd been auctioned, and the two men who took her home for a week both found themselves strangled with a barbed wire on the first night while she'd used the bathroom. She'd come out to see him placing a black eternal rose on the countertop, along with a set of clothes she could change into, his mismatched eyes locking with hers before he'd left. The rose, the prettiest thing she had ever seen, all black and frozen in time, had been the first gift she remembered receiving, the clothes the softest fabric to touch her skin. She had taken them both with her.

It had happened again the third time in a sex club, and the fourth, and the fifth, and again and again until she and the rest of the organizers knew—anyone who bid on her died. Yet, she brought in big money so she was put on the stage again and again, and he was there every time to take them out.

It had taken her a while to understand it was most likely game for him. A man who cared wouldn't have left her standing there naked, ready to be bought.

And yet, she stood there, worthless, discarded, unclaimed.

She shuddered as the black hole in her mind opened, beckoning her, calling her to fall into it and forget everything else, let everything about her existence be crushed out until nothing remained of herself.

The man's tongue touched her neck, and revulsion settled in the pit of her stomach, her hatred of her body intensifying as the black hole got closer and she hurtled toward it. Fifteen wouldn't care if she was catatonic, he wouldn't care if she wasn't there as long as her body was. But it had been years since someone had completely used her and she couldn't understand how this middle-aged monster got so close.

Where was he?

"Sir, you have to clear the balance before you can sample." The voice from the side, one of the auctioneers, cut through. The groping man straightened, giving her a moment of relief to collect herself.

Lyla took a step back, inhaling to control the spiral her thoughts were going toward, knowing she would lose herself if she went in, but it was a struggle to resist.

The man handed a wad of cash to the auctioneer, and Lyla surveyed the club again, trying to see if the devil was there.

He wasn't.

Swallowing down the bitter disappointment, she tried to come up with a way she could get out of the night mostly intact.

"Let's go, sweetheart." Fifteen settled his arm around her waist and she looked at the wedding band on his finger, wondering if his wife knew he was out with the intention of fucking a girl half his age. But it was none of her business. They dug their graves, and she felt no remorse when they fell into it.

As they made their way outside, her heart began to pound.

Outside.

She *loved* the outside.

But she didn't see it, not much. Growing up, her childhood and teenage years had been spent in special training houses. Some had been underground, some above, but they had always been confined within, her bed in the basement with the other kids. Now, she lived in a dormitory of other girls, in a complex that was large and heavily protected, but they weren't allowed to go outside without reason and escort. That was one of the only reasons she looked forward to the auction, because if someone won her, she would get some respite for a moment outside, feel the wind and see the sky, if only for a brief moment.

The man led her out the backdoor of the club into the alley that opened into the parking lot.

"Stay here while I get my car," Fifteen instructed her. "I don't have to tell you what will happen if you try to run, do I?"

She shook her head. She knew what they did to those who ran. Her only other friend had run away when they'd been children, and she knew to this day they were hunting her. The Syndicate, the organization who owned all the slaves, did not let anyone escape. She had run one time too, and she'd been caught. And she had experienced first-hand what they did to those who ran.

Shoving the memory away, she stayed where she was. At her easy acquiescence, he smiled and left.

Standing alone at the edge of the alley behind the building, Lyla turned her neck up for the glimpse of the night sky, her heart heavy at seeing nothing but the dark. She knew the stars weren't visible in the city some nights, she'd just hoped they would be. It had been too long since she had seen them, and too little in her short but hard life. But there was nothing tonight, no moon, no stars, just endless black littered by gray smoke and clouds.

She wondered some days what the point of her existence even was, on days when the future looked as the sky did—bleak, hopeless, endless. But then she reminded herself of the one thing that kept her going, the search for one little answer that made her wake up every morning and brave the day.

Suddenly, the hair on the back of her neck rose.

It was his scent that reached her first, a scent she'd only inhaled a few times in all the years he'd watched her, a scent that had imprinted itself in her mind. She'd only been so close to him a few times, and she didn't know exactly what he smelled like because she hadn't scented many nice things in her life, but it was distinct and male, and it was *him.*

She knew he was behind her. She could feel his breath on the top of her head, feel the heat of his larger body at her back, feel her dormant senses flaring to life as they always did in contact with him. And having him at her back always made her feel both chased and cherished, the dichotomy of emotions difficult for her to comprehend herself.

God, she hated him, she hated her response to him, hated that she wanted to hate him deeper but couldn't, and she hated that he knew it and didn't care one bit.

She stayed still, not breaking the silence with a single word. She had asked him the question a few times, and each time he had fucked with her mind, and left her confused, frustrated, and angry. She just held onto the anger now, as she had for many years. Anger was good. Anger made her *feel.* Anger reminded her that she was still alive.

"Did you enjoy his touch?"

The voice, *his* voice, came quietly from behind her. If death had a voice, it would be his. Again, she didn't know what his voice was similar to, because she didn't have anything to compare it to. But she knew she'd heard the voices of many men in her life, and his was, without a doubt, the *most dangerous* of them all.

It reminded her of a vague story she remembered someone telling her, a memory that was faded and probably from before she got into this life—the story of a man playing pipes and making all the rodents in town follow him, right off the edge of a cliff to their deaths, happily and merrily as they danced along. He had that kind of a voice—deep, alluring, seductive, a voice that could lead people obliviously to a cliff and to their own demise, making them enjoy it while they remained blind. A dangerous, dangerous voice on a dangerous, dangerous man. The voice of death beckoning the mortals to test their mortality.

It was just her luck that she had found him, of all people, that fateful night years ago.

She kept silent, refusing to follow to his tune.

"I asked you a question, *flamma,*" he reminded her again.

So did I, she wanted to say.

She didn't know why he called her that. She was sure he knew her name, and was even more certain it was as close to a term of endearment as a man like him could get. In the beginning, when he'd called her that, it had filled her with hope and made her feel a sense of belonging. As the hope dwindled, she knew it meant nothing. It grated on her. She wasn't his *anything.* A man like him wasn't endeared to anything.

She grit her teeth, her jaw locking in place, the urge to turn around and look at him acute in her body. But she knew his games, and she knew the best thing she could do was not play along. He wanted her reactions and withholding them gave her the power, at least momentarily.

'You will never hear my voice again. Go to fucking hell!'

The memory danced across her mind, the last time she had been alone with him, her failed attempts of getting answers from him having led to an angry promise. Up until now, she was proud of not having uttered a word to him.

A silver car came to a stop in front of the alley.

Taking a deep breath, ignoring the man at her back who was clearly hidden since there was no reaction from Fifteen, the man who had purchased her for the night, she walked to the car. Getting into the passenger seat, she strapped herself in, hating her translucent robe and the way Fifteen looked at her. They all looked at her but no one saw her, none except the man who watched her like it was his religion.

She turned to look out the window where he stood, barely making out the silhouette of his body. A lighter came to life in his hand, momentarily making him visible. She watched as he played with the lighter, before looking up, their gazes locking as the car began to move.

"Can't wait to fuck you tonight, sweetheart," the monster at her side chuckled.

She held her tongue, resisting the urge to tell him the only penetration tonight would be a bullet in his body.

CHAPTER 3

LYLA

There was something about seeing someone die that she could never get used to. No matter how many times she'd seen it at this point, it always jolted her when it happened. A normal, moral person would feel shock and grief and disgust and fear. Yet she, possibly because she knew these men were the bottom of the barrel, felt nothing but relief, and even vengeance to a degree. The only sadness she felt was for the families. She imagined a wife wondering why her husband hadn't come home, only to find out he was out cheating and screwing a sex slave behind her back. That was fucking sad. She felt more for a woman she'd never met than she did for the man in front of her.

The shot came in through the window, through the monster's hand that had been about to touch her again, blood splattering on the white walls of the hotel suite. The monster screamed, shaking his hand that had a hole in it.

The bullet missed her by inches, and yet her heart never once raced or thought to dive away to save herself like it once had. Of all the things *he* had and hadn't done, physically endangering or hurting her had never been one of them.

The man in front of her grabbed her by the other arm, suddenly turning her to the glass window, using her body as a shield, which was frankly stupid because she was short and petite and his head was way above hers.

That was exactly where the second bullet went through.

The man fell down, his eyes vacant, dead to the world in a split second.

He was the fifteenth.

Sighing, Lyla looked down at the blood on herself and went to the bathroom, shutting the door. She knew the drill. She knew a call would go to security and her handler, that someone would come and escort her back to the housing complex the girls lived in and all of it would take about twenty minutes. Those twenty minutes were precious. They were *hers.*

She threw the damned translucent robe to the side and stepped into the bath. She had never had baths until she started being auctioned and men brought her to the hotel. It was close to the club, owned by whoever ran the whole operation, and just easier for people to slake their lusts at immediately after a purchase.

She didn't know who ran the operations, none of the girls did. But she knew it was called The Syndicate, only because she had once served at a meeting where they had talked about it and she had eavesdropped. On the ground though, they had handlers who had handlers, who also had handlers, and she didn't know how high the chain of command went. She was just at the lowest rung of the pyramid, given a hotel to be used at. This was where all short-term purchases were taken care of. Long-term contracts meant moving somewhere else, wherever the buyer wanted.

The hotel catered rooms to every kind of debauched desire, the most rampant being non-consensual sex. But if a fetish existed, it was catered to. There was no concept of consent and legality, no empathy or morality. It was an abyss of nothingness.

She had been to many of the rooms in the hotel, and all of them had an en-suite bath that she always made use of, even if for just five minutes. Those five minutes were special. She cherished that time of being alone from eyes and relatively safe.

The tub filled to the brim and she went underwater, blessed silence encompassing her, her eyes closing, her breathing on pause. She gripped the side of the tub with her fingers, the black hole beckoning again, so close. Over the years, the hole had gotten larger and larger, its pull more intense than it had been. She would not get a chance like this again, the ultimate escape, the ultimate defiance of everyone who took pieces of her, leaving her hollow on the inside, until she could feel nothing.

Under the water, in the silence, she didn't have to be anything. She didn't have to know who she was. She *didn't* know who she was. She didn't know what she liked or didn't like, or what she would choose if she was a normal person with a normal life. Would she be an artist or a doctor or a dancer or something else? Would she have loving parents, brothers and sisters, family that loved her and worried for her if she didn't return home on time? Would she care for them or would she be selfish? What would her hobbies be? Would she like cats or dogs or none? Would she have allergies? Would she have a partner who loved her? Would sex actually be something pleasurable or something she dreaded? Were people on the outside ever raped? Would she be free?

Her lungs began to burn, the urge to let them burn out filling her, to let it all go, to let it all end once and for all.

It would be so easy to let go.

But she had to live.

For that one answer *he* held.

One more day. If she made it one more day, she could worry about the day afterward later.

Taking a massive gulp of air, she came out of the tub, her chest heaving as oxygen rushed into her bloodstream, her hair dripping as her eyes moved to the corner of the bathroom. The door she had locked was open.

He stood there.

That gave her pause. Twice in one night?

Why the fuck was he there? He didn't really make himself known after a kill. This was unprecedented. But she wasn't going to talk to him, much less give him the satisfaction of a reaction. He was cold and manipulative. Just because he was fixated on her didn't mean a thing.

Under the muted yellow lights of the bathroom, he was more visible to her than he had been in a while. She took him in, her eyes taking in his vision. He was rich, she knew that much, not just because of his clothes. He was wearing all black like every single time she'd seen him. It probably helped him blend into the shadows—a three piece suit sans the tie, the shirt opened to give a glimpse of his masculine chest.

He wasn't the best-looking man she had seen. No, she had seen many, many more beautiful men. But he was, *without a doubt*, the most dangerous-looking. Maybe it was the way his jaw was carved, shadowed with a dark scruff that seemed to perpetually be the same length. Or maybe it was his frame—tall, wide, muscled in the sleek way of a combative panther. Or maybe it was the stillness, his sheer ability to lock and focus on something so intently it made him feel like a weapon of death. Or maybe, it was those eyes—one utter black, the other an odd combination of green and gold—hypnotic, ensnaring, lethal, a duality of death and afterlife within one gaze.

Maybe it was none of those things. Maybe it was just the fact that she had seen him murder people without an iota of emotion for so long, she just associated danger with him.

The reason she knew he was rich, however, was simply because there was no way he could have the access to the clubs and every other part of this seedy underworld that he did unless he had money. Only two kinds of people had that access—slaves or buyers, and he was the farthest thing from a slave she'd ever seen. Though she didn't know if he was a buyer, if he had his own sex slave or a harem of them serving his every need.

The idea left a rotten taste in her mouth. With everything he did on the side while also stalking her, she wondered if he got the time. And why he did what he did, why no one knew him, or who he was outside of it, she didn't know. She didn't know a thing about him despite knowing him for years, and despite being one of the only people to have seen his face.

Feeling older than her twenty-four years, tired to the bone of simply breathing, she kept her face steady, breaking their gazes and looking into the water.

"Eyes."

The slow, deliberate command of a word speared through her body. She clenched her jaw, not understanding what he was doing here, and why he was speaking to her when he had never said what she wanted to hear.

"I won't ask again."

Something in the tone of his voice, like an underside of a blade, cut through her confusion, making the small part inside her that knew he was dangerous instinctively react. It reminded her of the handler she'd had when she'd been fourteen, training her in the art of obedience for the right man. She had learned, not through obedience but through fear.

She turned her neck to look at him again, her gaze locking with his devilish mismatched eyes, waiting, a sliver of fear in her body lingering after the memory of her adolescent training.

He tilted his head to the side. "Afraid of me, *flamma?*"

The knuckles on her hands turned white with her grip. No, she wasn't afraid of him. Or maybe she was. He elicited vastly different responses in her.

"Won't you give me your voice? Even if I give you your answer?"

The question was soft, but effective enough to make her heart begin to thud. Would he answer her? Or was he toying with her? From the look on his face, she couldn't tell.

"Will you?" she finally gave in, speaking to him for the first time in months, swallowing as the man with her answers stood still against the wall.

"One day."

Bitter disappointment crashed into her, followed on its heels by rage, her words falling from her lips in a barrage she had been keeping in for so long. "You're worse than these monsters. You dangle hope and take it away every single time." She turned her face, her lips quivering, hating the ease at which she cried, the ease with which she felt. "Stay away from me. I want nothing to do with you."

He stayed still beside the sink, leaning against the wall, casual but alert, his devilish gaze steady on her as she resumed her silence.

"They will be here in a few minutes," he told her, shifting topics at her continued, deliberate silence.

She already knew that. That wasn't news.

"I want you to tell them what happened." He straightened from the wall he'd been leaning against as he spoke. "Tell them the Shadow Man was here."

Why?

She almost asked but bit her tongue, her gaze wary as she looked at the man almost the entire underworld was terrified of, and for good reason. His entire expression stayed neutral the way it mostly did, but his eyes gleamed. He didn't answer her silent question, refusing to acknowledge it just like she refused to voice it.

She watched as his hand went to his inner jacket pocket, bringing out a black eternal rose, putting it on the counter beside the sink. "If I stay away from you, you'll miss me, *flamma.*"

Fuck him.

She wanted to ask him why he left those for her, why that specific rose, why specifically after a kill. She had fifteen of them now, an entire bouquet worth that she kept hidden in a box lest someone steal it. As twisted as it was, they were the only gift she had ever received, and she was possessive of them, along with the clothes he brought her every time.

She looked around to see where the bag of clothes was, her search coming up empty. Nothing. There wasn't a bag.

Her eyes went up to him, fire flooding her veins. He was playing with her again. Why? What satisfaction did he get from inciting her reactions, toying with her emotions?

One corner of his mouth slashed up in a half-smirk. He knew she had come to rely on him bringing her clothes, clothes she wore back to the complex, clothes she washed and kept safe because they were the nicest she owned that were only *hers.* She didn't know if she was just easy to read and no one had tried it before, or if it was his special skill at deciphering her, but he knew her thought patterns and she absolutely *hated* that.

Without another word, he left the bathroom, closing the door behind himself, and Lyla got up, wrapping a towel around her body. She was mad at him, mad at herself, mad at the world. And she knew she only had five more minutes to be mad before she had to be docile again, before she would give up on her anger, and that just made her angrier.

Marching out of the bathroom, she came to a sudden stop at seeing a plain paper bag on the bed. Ignoring the corpse on the side of the room, she rushed to the bag and saw a pair of black jeans, a white sleeveless top, a pair of nude cotton bra and panties that looked comfortable. Taking the tags off, she quickly donned the pieces, yet again questioning how he knew her exact sizes for everything. It was a perfect fit. And he had been testing her to see her reaction.

Hair still wet from the bath, she towel dried it as something on the table beside the bed caught her eye.

A phone.

She stared at it for a long minute, a gaping hole in her chest. Someone else could have stolen it and asked for help. She couldn't. She didn't have anyone she could call. And calling the police was out of the question. With the kind of people she knew were involved in these operations, she would either end up dead by an organizational assassination or dead by a police encounter. There was nowhere for her to go, not until she got what she needed from the one man who refused to give her answers.

Turning away from the phone, she looked at herself in the mirror. A short, petite frame with ripe breasts, as her handler had told her. Hair so red and wavy, falling to her waist, surrounding a circular face with softness, light freckles on her nose, naturally arched red brows over bright green eyes that looked almost blue in some lights. She was beautiful; she had been told many times. But when she looked at the mirror, it wasn't her beauty she saw. She saw her only tie to her past, and she saw questions. Did her genetics come from her parents or grandparents? Were they alive or dead? Did they have eyes like hers or another color?

As she continued to dry her hair with the towel, she imagined all the scenarios, and none of them brought her any comfort at all. But her mind rarely, if ever, did bring her comfort.

The sound of the door opening had her throwing the towel to the side as she sat down on the bed, doing her best to appear meek, her hands folded in her lap, her head bent as she watched from under her eyelashes.

Two security guys came in, armed to the teeth, and looked at the dead body before eyeing her.

"What the fuck happened?"

What always happened.

He'd told her to tell them, but these guards were new and she didn't want to risk their extra attention. So, she said what she always said. "I don't know. I was in the bathroom."

They believed her, not that they had any reason not to.

One of the guys, a dark-haired man who looked scary in his seriousness, nodded at her. "Grab your stuff. We have to get you back."

Taking the bag the clothes had come in, she went to the bathroom to grab the rose and the small bottles of free toiletries. She always took those. The small bottles were pretty and, more often than not, they smelled amazing.

Roving an eye around the bedroom to see if anything else was worth taking, she followed the guys out within minutes. They took her down the elevator straight into the parking lot, and then straight into the unmarked sedan. Within minutes, she was locked in and they pulled out into the city.

"So," the driver began. "What exactly happened up there?"

His skeptic tone wasn't lost on her. But she didn't know him, and there was no way she was talking. She'd learned early on that talking to outsiders got her punishment and nothing more.

"Exactly what I said."

The guy stayed silent for a second. Something was off about him. She didn't know what it was. She didn't say anything else, just looked out the window and watched the city pass as they headed to the outskirts.

It was sad that she didn't even know what the city was called or where the complex was. They never told any of the girls where they were moved. She could have been moved within the same city all her life or hopped a handful, she didn't know. She wondered sometimes where she would live if she were ever free. She knew there were mountains and seas in the world, but she'd never seen either. She would like mountains. They would make her feel secure, like tall guards standing all around her, keeping her safe from outside invasion. Yeah, she'd like to see mountains one day.

And she most likely never would.

Blinking the stinging feeling in her eyes, she kept her face neutral.

"I've heard guys who bid on you die. That true?" the burly man from the passenger side asked.

She didn't respond. There was nothing for her to respond. The rumor mill was working as it always did. And it didn't do shit for her.

Before he could say another word, the familiar fences of the complex came into view, the large gates opening to let them in, imprisoning her once again.

CHAPTER 4

LYLA

The complex was large, a gated piece of land in the middle of nowhere with four buildings. One building housed security personnel and the handlers on site, the remaining three housed girls of all ages. Building A had dormitories and training areas for girls under ten, Building B had the same for all girls aged ten to eighteen, and Building C—the one where she lived—had slightly larger dormitories and one medical room. Though it was a normal room, it had been dubbed so by the girls because that's where they were sent if one of them came back too injured. It was the nicest room she had ever slept in, with a proper bed instead of the bunk beds they were given, and a soft mattress and two pillows. Her mattress was hard and her single pillow harder. Although it didn't matter because usually when someone went to the medical room, they were in too much pain to notice any of the nice things.

She had been there once since she'd come to the complex—the night she'd met *him*.

She swallowed, shaking herself out of the painful memory, one that had sent her to the room for weeks to heal, one that had almost convinced her she was going to die.

Getting out of the car as the security people closed the gates, she made her way toward her housing and watched her handler, Three, come down the stairs from Building C. The girls didn't know the handlers' real names. Most of them didn't even know their own real names. They were all given names, and that's who they became. Three had been her handler since she came to the complex at sixteen, for eight years. The woman was usually not as bad as handlers One and Two were. She was fair to the girls, wanted them fed and rested and looking good, and had simple rules for her dorms. As long as one toed the line, she was decent. But Lyla wasn't fooled by the charade. She knew how quickly the switch flipped, how little time it took for calm to become cruel.

The older woman, at least in her forties, looked down at Lyla with a frown on her face. "Again?"

Lyla nodded. The question hadn't even needed to be fully asked. After six years, they were all aware of the bad luck she brought her buyers. Everyone knew someone targeted them, but no one knew who.

Three shook her head. "Idiot men, they never learn."

Lyla stayed silent, waiting for instruction. She didn't have to wait long.

"Go, get rest."

Without waiting for more, Lyla quickly skirted the other woman and climbed the stairs to the building. It was a few decades old, the paint peeling in some places and the furniture cracked in some, but it was still the nicest house she had been in. Complexes like these were many, and Lyla had lived in five different complexes—the most unusual for any girl—for some bizarre reason. Usually, a girl stayed where she was initially sent, getting familiar with the location and the handlers. She might be moved once, or maximum twice, but never five times, and Lyla didn't understand why she had been. She'd been a compliant child, a quiet adolescent, and it just didn't make sense. She was just glad she'd been steady for the last eight years.

Climbing the stairs to the second floor where her room was, she passed a few girls loitering on the landing, talking to each other about their customers or masters, whichever they had. There weren't as many girls in this building as the others, mainly because a lot of girls were contracted for long-term and had to stay with their contractors. Just like her friend Malini had been for a few months.

She and Malini hadn't been close, not until the night that had changed her life and the other girl had stood by her, letting her scream as she held her hand. In the aftermath of that event, Lyla had found the closest thing to a friend for the first time, and it had made breathing a little easier for a while.

Opening the door to her room, she walked in to find both of her roommates locked in a heated kiss, pulling apart when she entered.

"Sorry, I'll come back later," she told them.

"Nah, it's fine," the taller one of the couple, Reina, spoke. "We heard you got bid on again."

Lyla hesitated before entering and going to her small bed in the corner, collapsing on it. "Yes."

"Is he dead?" the other roommate, Millie, asked.

"Yes."

"Damn," Reina muttered, climbing the bunk bed to get on the top. "How?"

Lyla pointed to her forehead. "Bullet to the head."

"Girl, I'd just about give anything for your stalker to be obsessed with me right now," Millie remarked, the tinge of envy clear in her voice. "Any man near me dying? No fucking anyone? The best kinda life."

"It's not just any man," Reina reminded her. "He's a killer. Sorry, but I'd take rich pricks any day over him. With rich pricks, I know what I'm getting. I can handle that."

"But can you imagine . . ."

Lyla tuned out the conversation, closing her eyes and lying flat on the bed, not wanting to hear what they had to say. They didn't like her. They lived with her, tolerated her, but she wasn't their friend. They didn't look out for her like they looked out for their actual friends. She didn't know why, but that was just the way it was. For some reason, nobody had wanted to be her friend in all the years. The one friend she'd had in childhood had left her behind and run away, and Malini had left now too.

And she was *tired.*

Without changing, she simply climbed under her thin sheet and turned to the wall, giving her back to her roommates.

The wet sound of kissing filled the room like it did a lot of the nights, and Lyla simply tuned it out. All the girls got trained with both men and women, and many of them found companionship with each other as they grew up. It was perfectly natural in her world, and she was glad that Reina and Millie had each other. In the fucked up world they lived in, it was a boon to find something like this.

For her, there was nothing.

She had lain in countless beds and been used against her will, nowhere to escape but in her mind. Sometimes, her body had reacted, sometimes it hadn't. Sometimes, it had been painful, sometimes it hadn't. She'd thought that was the worst that could happen to her, and yet the threat of worse always lingered.

She felt dead inside, the only spark of life brought on by the man in the shadows, and even that she didn't know if it was because of their history or because of attraction.

As the breathing behind her got heavier, Lyla closed her eyes and wondered about him. Why was he fixated on her? Why give her black eternal roses for every kill? Why have a conversation with her now and instruct her to tell everyone it was him? Why did he do anything he did? The more she thought about him, the more pissed she became. And it was exhausting to have her emotions sway from anger to depression, a constant back and forth.

Somehow, maybe because of the exhaustion, she felt herself slowly drifting, her last thought of the hypnotic mismatched eyes and a feeling of danger chasing her.

She woke with a start as someone shook her.

Blinking rapidly to focus her eyes, she saw Reina's concerned face looking down at her. "Three has called you to the office."

Dread pooled in her stomach.

The office was never used, not unless someone from higher up in the operation was visiting and wanted to hold meetings.

And they were calling her.

Fuck.

Swallowing to wet her suddenly dry throat, she swung her legs around and straightened, her hair a nest falling around her body. "Did she say why?"

"No."

Okay, this wasn't good. But she knew it was coming. She might be bringing them money but she was losing their clients permanently. That wasn't good for business. They were either going to send her away or simply kill her, and the bone-tired weariness inside her almost felt relieved at the thought of the latter.

Without wasting any more time, she walked out of the room in the same clothes she'd slept in, the now wrinkled clothes that he had given her, and stepped out of the building into daylight. She barely took a breath of air before a guard was quickly escorting her to the main building, not even granting her a split second of reprieve to feel the sun on her face.

Straightening her clothes, she made her way into the building, following the guard as he turned left into a corridor, leading her toward the last door down the path. Despite the daylight outside, the corridor was dark and damp, a musty smell inside that seemed to emanate from the walls themselves.

He opened the door and nodded for her to enter.

Taking a deep breath, she went in.

And froze.

Three stood in the corner, an older man sat behind the desk, and *he* occupied the chair at the front.

What the hell was he doing there?

She stayed still, keeping her face as neutral as she could, and faced Three.

The older woman indicated the only empty chair in the room, in front of the desk and beside *his*. Heart pounding, she gingerly sat in it.

"This is Mr. H," Three spoke in the way of introduction, indicating the older man behind the desk looking at her with a scowl on his face, his beady eyes making her distinctly uncomfortable. "You know why he's here."

Lyla nodded.

"Speak up, girl!" Mr. H's voice boomed, making her jolt with the sudden loudness. Heart racing, she willed herself to calm down, hating that *he* would hear her voice again when she'd told him he wouldn't. The fact that Three hadn't introduced him even though he was there made her wonder if she even knew who he was. Did Mr. H know? Did anyone?

"I . . . I don't know what to say," she told the older man quietly, deliberately ignoring the dark presence on the side.

"For a start, tell me how last night happened," the older, creepy man instructed.

Ignoring the way *his* eyes were burning on her, but aware of what he'd asked her to say, she addressed Mr. H. "It was the Shadow Man."

Three gasped.

It was fascinating, seeing the way the older man's scowl faded, replaced with something very akin to fear. She knew the Shadow Man was a rumor in the underworld, but to witness just the impact the sound of his name could have on someone powerful like Mr. H made something warm twist in her belly.

For the first time in her life, she understood what the barest glimpse of power felt like. And she wondered if it gave him a rush, to be there and witness it in person, to see how people reacted to his name, oblivious to the fact that he was right there.

Maybe that was why *he* had come. To find some twisted satisfaction in their terror.

Mr. H leaned forward. "How the fuck do you know that?"

What could she say to that? Thinking quickly on her feet, she answered with as much earnestness as she could muster. "There was a call on the phone after the buyer was shot. The man on the other side introduced himself as the Shadow Man."

Mr. H frowned. "That's very strange. Not a part of his M.O."

She didn't comment on that.

As he contemplated in silence, she felt a gloved hand touch hers, the man at her side slipping something into her hand. Paper, from the feel of it. Fisting her hand, she surreptitiously stuffed it in her jeans pocket to look at later, confused as to what was going on.

Mr. H stared at her in a discomforting way for a long time before steeping his fingers, resting his elbows on the desk. "You present quite the conundrum, girl. You get some of our highest bids and lose us some of our best clients."

Lyla stayed silent, not sure if and how to address this. She focused on the man speaking, aware of the man silent at her side, and felt an odd feeling of safety envelop her. Odd, because it wasn't an emotion she was familiar with. She might not know anything about him, but she knew he wouldn't let her be killed for his own reasons. His presence there ensured she stay alive.

A sudden slight gleam entered Mr. H's dark eyes. "Alright, that's all. You can go now."

Lyla didn't know what the change meant, but she doubted it was anything good. Taking that as dismissal, she stood up and walked out of the office, the guard waiting to escort her back to her room.

Thankfully, the room was empty, both Reina and Millie somewhere away. Sitting on her unmade bed, she took the crumpled piece of paper out from her pocket, looking at the note he had passed her, a masculine string scrawl of a sentence that made her breath catch.

'Your voice makes my atoms sing.'

She didn't understand the rush she felt at those words. It was . . . beautiful. Almost poetic, and she wouldn't have called him poetic in her wildest dreams. But was he just saying it to soften her or did he mean it? She didn't know but she knew she shouldn't feel that rush, especially not when it was coming from him. But sitting alone in her room, she couldn't deny it affected her. *He* affected her, no matter how much she tried to resist. Over the years, she had gone from hopefully opening herself up to his impact on her, to accepting it, to denying it, to resisting it, to hating it, and repeat. A cycle rooted in the fact that she wanted him completely but didn't know if he returned the feeling beyond keeping her safe.

And she was exasperated—with him and herself and their twisted relationship.

But he'd never given her a note before. *What was he up to?*

Getting up, she went to her locker and took out the box from the back. Opening it to all the black eternal roses she'd saved over the years, some dried and wilted, some comparatively fresher, she placed the note inside with them, hating herself slightly more for keeping them all. Tucking the box at the back again, she locked up and went to freshen up, knowing she had a few hours before starting her shift.

After using the communal showers, she dressed in shorts and a tank top, tied her hair up in a bun, and went down to the kitchen to eat something. There weren't many options to choose from, but they did feed everyone, and frankly, that was more than enough on most days. The kitchen was busy with girls taking their meals, some of them talking to each other, most of them keeping to themselves like she did. It was common. Something was broken within every single one of them, and while that was a point of commonality, it wasn't a point of companionship.

Keeping her head down, she got some milk and cereal in a cheap plastic bowl, and went back upstairs to the solace of her room before she had to start work in a few hours. When she wasn't being auctioned for short- or long-term contracts, she worked as a server in the Club District, rotating in The Syndicate nightclubs, strip clubs, and sex clubs, sometimes even as a dancer if they needed more girls on stage. She got groped and whistled at and couldn't keep any of the tips she made, but it was still better than a lot of the other girls had it. There were girls who got drugged and got fucked on a daily basis for videos sold on the dark web; sex slaves who lived with masters so cruel their lives were horror stories, children who were made to do things no child ever should. And it wasn't just girls. She knew there was a whole operation like this one for young boys too. If there was a buyer in the market, they were catered to with whatever they needed. So, she truly felt lucky that her daily job was only limited to unwanted attention and groping.

And yet, despite telling herself that she was luckier, she felt cursed.

Her eyes went to the knife and an apple on Reina's small desk, her mind swaying again. That was the thing she couldn't explain within herself. Sometimes, she caught sight of random, potentially lethal objects and immediately, her brain conjured up the image of what it would be like to use it on herself. That knife, for example, would be so easy, the sharp side of the blade going over the veins just once, so simple to put a full stop to it all. They would find her in the room, her white expensive shirt soaked in blood that matched her hair, a smile on her face for the first time as she said goodbye.

Closing her eyes, she put a stop to the fantasy, a slight tremor in her hand as she gripped her bowl.

Eat. Sleep. That's all.

That's all she needed to do. Sleep. Wake up. Repeat.

Just one more day.

Quickly finishing the last of her cereal, she climbed back into bed and slept again, quieting the demons in her head, at least for a bit, praying for a dream that would bring her some solace. And just her luck, she dreamed of him.

CHAPTER 5

LYLA, 1 YEAR AGO

He was there in one of the lounge areas, watching her with those devilish mismatched eyes of his as she danced on the stage at *Sanctum,* one of the more posh sex clubs in the Club District, catering to sex and socialization for the affluent under one roof. Aside from the back rooms, there were also rooms available for the night above the club at request.

It was one of the private parties for one of the higher ups, a private party of over a hundred men and women who came from powerful places—lawyers, judges, politicians, industrialists, mobsters, all of them mingling in a night of lustful celebrations.

People in various stages of undress were already scattered around the room, some fondling, some fucking. The more private ones took their chosen companion or companions for the night to the rooms in the back, ones that catered to all kinds of fetishes they could want to explore.

It had been a while since she'd seen *him,* physically seen him. She had felt him many times, known he'd been keeping an eye on her even more so, but actually seeing him wasn't usual. Her heart thud with each beat of the music as he watched her, and she focused on him, danced for him, just for him. Theirs was an odd relationship, if it could even be called that.

She had found him accidentally on a fateful night, and he had helped her out. She had never believed that she would see him again afterward, not until he showed up at one of the clubs where she'd been serving drinks one night. She had pretended not to know him, and he had pretended not to look at her. They'd both been lying. Since then, for years, he had become a constant presence in her life, an anchor she had become emotionally dependent on even though she knew she shouldn't be. He was dangerous, he was manipulative, and he enjoyed playing with her emotions a little too much. And yet, when he came seeking her, she was found.

"Hey doll," someone shouted from below her, breaking her trance. She looked down to find Three's supervisor, the main handler for the entire housing complex, calling her. She descended the steps behind the stage, walking to the supervisor.

"That's some very important clients." He pointed to the lounge area where *he* was sitting with a few other men, most already with companions from the many girls available. "Go make sure they're entertained."

Heart pounding, she gave a nod and sashayed toward the lounge area. It was slightly elevated from the rest of the club, with plush maroon and brown couches scattered around an oval glass table, the lighting there dimmer than they were elsewhere.

One of the older men on a couch, already sitting with a semi-naked girl on his lap, grinned at her. "Aren't you a looker . . . Come to join us, sweetheart?"

Before she could respond, a voice, *his* voice, dryly inserted a sharp comment. "Your heart won't be able to handle more than one, Landon."

The older man, Landon, chuckled, evidently the sharpness going over his head. "You're right. Sweetheart, why don't you entertain Mr. Blackthorn instead?"

Mr. Blackthorne.

Was that even his actual name or an alias? Whatever it was, it was *fitting*.

Breaths becoming rapid, she turned to the man on the couch, aware of the way his eyes dissected her barely-there golden sequin dress.

Putting one leg on each side of his, close enough to feel the heat of his body for the first time, she straddled him as she did any man about to get a lap dance. But her heart never pounded the way it did as she straddled him, her hands finding his broad shoulders, tentatively steadying herself as she began to move her hips to the music.

Their gazes locked.

Her eyes drifted to his mouth, the slash of pressed lips as he simply sat, appearing unbothered.

But she could see the darkening of his pupil in his lighter eye, could feel the solid bulge in his pants, getting harder the more she moved.

She ground against him, and suddenly, both her arms were behind her, held tightly in a steel grip, his other hand holding her jaw, reminiscent of the way he'd held her in the maze that first time. Breathing heavily, her breasts heaving, almost falling out of her minuscule dress, she watched him as a male singer's vocals crooned in the background.

The hand holding her jaw moved to her mouth.

Gloves. He was wearing leather gloves. So odd, but again so fitting with him.

His fingers traced her lips, and her mouth parted. She didn't kiss, had never wanted to kiss anyone and thankfully no one had forced her to. That was something that was only hers, no one else's. If someone tried to get her mouth, she simply distracted them. She didn't know why she held onto that, maybe because it was the only thing she could hold onto that left her with any semblance of control in a world spinning out of it. Whatever it was, it was just hers. And she'd never wanted to give it away more.

He leaned forward, his lips moving to her ear, and she held her breath. "I have plans for tonight and you're ruining them, *flamma.*"

The heat that had been simmering in her body suddenly died a cold death.

His plans.

Of course.

She closed her eyes, calling on her strength. How could she have forgotten who he was, how he toyed with her for his own purpose?

Although embarrassment wasn't an emotion she felt often—with the kind of life she had, there wasn't really any room for it—she felt the flush heating her face as she struggled to get up and walk away.

He held her still, her hands behind her back, her breasts thrust into his chest, her neck tilted for his nose. She had been trying to . . . she didn't know what she'd been trying to do. She hadn't wanted to seduce him, not really, but she'd wanted to be close to him, to feel him against herself, but not necessarily in a sexual way. Though she was aroused, it had been the . . . safety she'd been enjoying. Even as he held her immobile, she didn't feel the familiar panic she would've been feeling had it been another man.

She'd been trying to create intimacy, and he had been thinking about his plans.

Not good for any girl's morale.

She'd promised him he wouldn't hear her voice again, so she kept quiet, focusing on the light at the back, steadying her breaths.

"Are you angry, *flamma?*" he asked into her neck. If she didn't know better, she'd say he was amused. But she did know better, and she knew he didn't feel things like she did. Amusement was beyond his range of emotion, probably. Maybe not. She didn't know.

She stayed silent and tried to pull away.

His grip on her wrists tightened. "Your emotions will get you killed here."

He said that as though she was afraid of dying. If someone pointed a gun at her head, she would probably welcome the bullet.

And the devil that he was, he knew her thoughts. "How will you find your answers if you don't live, hmmm?"

Fucking bastard.

He was holding answers hostage over her head, forcing her to continue to live. He had been doing it for years. Every time she'd asked him about that night, he told her she would get the answer one day if she continued to live. The last time she'd asked him had been a year ago, and absolutely done with his bullshit, she had taken the one thing from him she knew he enjoyed in their limited encounters—her voice.

But he knew she wouldn't let go without knowing, and he used it mercilessly, forcing her to shake off dark thoughts, forcing her to see another night, forcing her to live another day. She hated him for it.

His breath fell over her neck, slowly on her pulse, before he pulled back, locking their gazes together.

"The world isn't ready to see who I would become if this—" his thumb pressed on her pounding pulse "—ever stops."

Lyla stared at him, and once again, marveled at how she would never understand him.

She wasn't important, and he was mistaken. If her heartbeat ever stopped, it wouldn't change a thing.

The next week, he was there again, the closest she'd come to seeing him in the span of a few days. He was there, and this time, a blonde half-naked girl was sitting on his lap.

Lyla froze in her step, the tray in her hand she was using as a server jostling with the sudden movement.

Something ugly, nasty swirled in her chest at the sight.

No.

She closed her eyes, taking a deep breath in before opening them again. The blonde was still there and the ugliness in her chest deepened. She knew it didn't make sense, that she had no rights and worse, no claims on this man. But he was *hers.* Whatever games he played, he played with *her.* It was *she* who was the object of his obsessions. She didn't want there to be another he was fixating on, another he was holding and worse, looking for with those eyes of his.

But she had no rights over him.

None.

Her hand holding the tray shook and she steadied it, reminding herself any spilled drinks would result in punishment.

The same men from last time sat around the lounge, and she kept her chin down, her fingers white at the vitriol inside her. The blonde flipped her hair over one shoulder, exposing her naked breasts to him, tugging on her nipples.

Lyla grit her teeth, placing the drinks on the table, purposely keeping her eyes down and neck turned away from him.

A man from the side, a younger, dark-haired guy smiled at her. "Why don't you come sit here, darling?"

Oh no.

Even though she didn't want to, she couldn't reject. That was one of the things servers were told to do—if a customer asked for something extra, you gave it to them. Thankfully, since the men who touched her had begun to die, the word on the street usually kept them away from her or making demands of her.

Gaze briefly flickering to the devil responsible for each death, she saw his face completely neutral, his eyes on the dancers onstage. With no cue from him on how to behave or what to do, she did the only thing she could without inviting punishment. She moved and tentatively sat down on the guy's lap, keeping her eyes fixed on a light away as he palmed her breasts. She didn't make a sound.

"Moan for me, darling."

She wouldn't. That was something she could control. She stayed silent, wondering if the devil would kill this one at all, since they were sitting together.

"Tough bitch," the man chuckled, clapping his hands to get the attention of the table. "A wager. Whoever gets her to moan gets a hundred thousand."

A few men whooped and her stomach dropped. She instinctively sought his gaze, only to find the mismatched eyes set on the man holding her.

"This one's trouble, boy," the older man who'd been there last week warned. "Better let her go before her guardian angel finds you."

The guy under her chuckled. "There are no angels in this place, old man."

No, but there were devils, the biggest of them looking at her.

"I'll make her moan."

Her heart stuttered at the sound of *his* voice as he tapped the blonde to get off him. She huffed and got up, finding another lap immediately.

The old man warned again. "She's not worth it, Blackthorne."

"Yes, she is," he stated, spreading his legs slightly and extending his gloved palm toward her.

Heart pounding, she walked to him, putting her hand in his gloved one.

He tugged her forward until she fell into his chest, his muscular leg between hers as he sat her down. Lyla stared at him, enthralled by the lights reflecting in his light golden-green eye and the complete lack of reflection in the black.

He put one hand on the back of the couch, the other going to the side of her thigh.

A shiver skittered down her spine at the simple touch, and it made no sense to her how one man's touch could light her up where other's failed to even spark. Maybe it was because of their history, their connection, their twisted relationship. Maybe it was because she was a fool to feel safe with him, even knowing there were multiple people behind her. Multiple men in a small dark space only ever incited fear in her. Right now, straddling his thigh, she felt anything but.

He tilted his head forward, lining his mouth with her ear, exactly as he had the previous week, and calmly asked, "Do you want me to cut his hand off or burn it?"

Lyla shuddered at his words, and not entirely in revulsion. Something inside her, something dark and deranged, wanted to see him do it, see him sever the hand that had touched her without her permission. And it scared her, that side of her.

She swallowed, basking in the power of that choice. "Cut it."

She felt him smile against her cheek, his breaths warm against her ear as he trapped her wrists in his wandering hand.

"Good girl."

The words, soft, full of praise, coming from him made something warm flood in her system, her hips grinding involuntarily, her movement limited, controlled by his body.

"And how do you want him to die?" he asked, his voice low, almost seductive. "Should the Shadow Man do it from a distance? Or up close and personal?" He pushed his thigh up on the last word.

He was talking about real murder and she was wet, so, so wet, more naturally wet than she'd ever been in her entire life. She hadn't even known she could lubricate so much, and the fact that something so gruesome was turning her on was disturbing. She was going to leave a spot on him.

"The slut is enjoying this!" The loud holler from the back made her stiffen, awareness falling inwith sharp blades on her consciousness.

"Shh." The words whispered against her ear soothed her frayed edges a bit. "It's just us. It's always just been us. Focus on me."

She closed her eyes and did as he asked. The noise of the club, the sounds of the men in the back, everything slowly fell away as she focused on the sound of his voice, the piper leading her to the cliff.

His nose went down the side of her neck. "He called you a slut. Are you a slut, *flamma?*"

She didn't know how to answer that, the loathing inside her rearing its head.

"Do you like my touch?" he asked, his grip on wrists firm as he brought his other hand to her mouth, tracing her lips.

"Yes," she breathed, his thumb dipping inside.

"If I pushed you down and filled you with my cock, would you enjoy it?"

Her pussy clenched at his words, the emptiness inside her acute. She gave a nod.

"Would you enjoy if someone else did it?"

Her body stiffened.

"Then you're my slut." His thigh pressed into her where she was empty, pressing her clit hard. *"Mine."*

Even though she hated the word, when he said it like that, something inside her bloomed. She would remember it. Next time someone called her a slut, she would remind herself of this moment.

"Now, moan for me and I'll give you a gift to take back."

A noise escaped her lips, completely unbidden, muffled as he pressed his thumb inside her mouth while she rode his leg, her movement limited because of the tight hold he had on her.

"Good girl." She felt the words against her neck just as he opened his mouth. Teeth scored her flesh and the multiple sensations from all over made her neck fall back, her lips clamping on his thumb as her body shuddered. His teeth on her neck sent heat through her entire body, an orgasm surprising her with its intensity, the stars behind her eyelids so beautiful she chased it for another second, holding onto them.

This was precious. A willing orgasm was so fucking precious.

Tears in her eyes, she blinked, looking up at the high ceiling.

Awareness filtered in slowly, the sound of laughter and music and chattering, and she looked down to find his gaze. For the first time in her memory, the aftermath of an orgasm didn't leave her feeling dirty, didn't leave her wanting to rip her own skin open.

She felt . . . pure. Precious. *Powerful.* All illusions, but she held on to them for a moment too.

His face remained neutral as it always did, the only sign that he had been affected in any way being the large bulge between his legs and the enlarged pupil in his light eye. He let go of her wrists and took his thumb out of her mouth, her teeth denting the gloves deeply. A throbbing sensation on her neck made her bring her hand up, touching the sensitive spot.

He'd marked her. For the first time, he'd visibly marked her.

In her experience, marks were never good. Marks meant pain and cruelty and carelessness. The mark he had given her had been pleasure and tenderness and deliberation. It was a gift, a claiming for her to remember she was his, that no one could get to her as long as he was there.

And to someone who had been owned but never belonged, it meant *everything*.

CHAPTER 6

LYLA, PRESENT DAY

Being back in *Sanctum* after months brought memories rushing to the surface for her. The last time she'd been there, he had marked her. It had filled her with hope again, and as time had passed, the hope had dwindled. Again.

She knew she needed to learn to keep her expectations in check, that she needed to accept her fate and her state of being without letting treacherous hope take over until she began to dream of more. But no matter how much she reminded herself of the same, it always happened unbidden. Hope was borne, hope died, and so did a little piece of her.

Shaking off her gloomy thoughts, she focused on the pain in her feet in the high heels. The club was particularly rowdy tonight. It wasn't a usual sex club, the kind that just catered to sex. No, it was a club that was the underbelly of operations. Dark deals, drugs, drinks, and dickheads were found in abundance there.

As she weaved her way through the crowd in the VIP lounge area of the single-level open space, the exact space where he'd made her moan, the balls of her feet ached in the platform heels all working girls had to wear. Her heart ached too because a year ago, she had been more full of hope than she was now, somehow expecting the moment to lead to something—an escape at the best, a deeper intimacy at the least.

It had led to nothing. Not a thing changed. He never touched her again but he continued his vigilance. And she was fucking *sick* of it.

He was clearly someone important within the underworld. She'd seen him make public appearances too many times since then, around too many powerful-looking people to question it. Mr. Blackthorne, as they called him, was someone important. He also walked the night as the Shadow Man, though she doubted anyone even suspected it. The Shadow Man was a hot, unhinged killer, thriving in the chaos he created. Mr. Blackthorne was cold, self-contained, and meticulous. If anyone suspected they were the same men, it was genius.

And she knew his secret. She could use it against him, threaten him with exposure, but she couldn't. She was weak and powerless, and the Shadow Man was the only being giving her a modicum of protection for whatever reason. She couldn't jeopardize that.

As she made her way through the club, she kept her face averted from that particular section. Even after years of tottering on the heels, she hadn't mastered them as perfectly as others. Something about walking in them made her feel more on display when all she wanted was to hide. She hated being on display when she longed for invisibility.

Completing an order of drugs and drinks to one of the tables where one of the servers was eating a well-dressed woman out, she turned to go back to the bar quickly when her eyes paused on Mr. H sitting in a dark corner of the section, talking to a man with light hair. She couldn't see his face, but from Mr. H's body language, the light-haired man seemed someone important.

Driven by some instinct she couldn't name, she headed to the alcove beside their table, eavesdropping.

"—and that's what I mean," Mr. H told the man, his voice low since the music was quieter in the VIP area. The light-haired man listened, the back of his head visible to her as he swirled the drink in his glass, a ring with some kind of snake symbol hefty on his right index finger.

"If it's him, we might finally have something," Mr. H continued. "If it's not, the girl is useless now anyway."

"The girl has more uses than you know of," the light-haired man replied in a cool tone. "But I hear you. He's been ... disruptive for too long."

"Sir," Mr. H leaned forward. "We can kill two birds with one stone. Let's make an example out of it."

The light-haired man gave a nod, and Mr. H grinned.

Lyla felt her blood run cold. Either they were talking about her or someone else who had recently become a problem for them. And she had a very strong feeling it was the former.

Before she could quietly move away, the light-haired man suddenly turned, his eyes coming to her in the corner. "Who do we have here?"

Lyla swallowed as Mr. H stood up and came to her, grabbing her by the arm and bringing her forward. "She's the one I was talking about."

The light-haired man with light brown eyes and a hook-like nose smirked, straightening in his seat. "Come, sit here, sweetheart."

No, she wanted to run. She wanted to go back to serving drinks.

But Mr. H had her in a tight grip, and she was trapped. Taking a deep breath, she took a step forward.

The light-haired man tugged her suddenly, making her fall into his lap. She tried to get up, struggling as he made her sit on him, chuckling while looking at Mr. H. "Get the drink."

Lyla turned sideways, watching in horror as Mr. H mixed some kind of blue powder in the stranger's remaining drink, handing the glass over to the man.

She began to struggle harder as the man restrained her with one hand, pushing the glass against her lips with the other. "Drink up like a good girl now."

The same words that had filled her with a rush filled her with nothing but dread. She sputtered, wriggling to get away when a sharp pain in her scalp had her stilling. Mr. H held her hair from the roots, almost pulling them out so tightly she whimpered in pain.

"No, please no!" she begged, hoping against hope that they would let her go.

"It's not for you, girl," the man she was sitting on chuckled again. "You're just the bait. It's to call *him* out. *Drink.*"

That somehow made it even worse.

In her moment of quiet, the glass tipped over in her mouth, bitter alcohol and something sour filling her until she had no choice but to swallow it down, the liquid burning her insides and settling uncomfortably in her stomach, some of it sputtering out of her mouth.

She felt sick, but they kept her immobile, making her down the entire drink.

And then they let her go.

She stood up and jerked away from them, stumbling in her heels, her balance completely off-center. Dizziness assaulted her, making her hold the wall for support, stars blinking in front of her eyes, her heart beginning to gallop like a wild horse, her entire body warming gradually to the point she began to sweat. Coherent thought began to leave her mind.

Light. She felt light, like the weight of the world had been taken from her shoulders, like there was nothing to worry about. What was this thing they had given her? She didn't know and didn't care. Her body began to sway in the rhythm of the music, her insides heating up and buoyant after endless drowning, a high hitting her so suddenly she didn't know what she would do when she crashed.

"Yeah, leave her like that. I want the hotel premises secure. She'll crash in a bit."

She heard the words but stayed in the alcove, dancing to the music, exhilarated and terrified as a small part of her retained sense, knowing this wasn't right.

No, she needed to get away.

Stumbling around the furniture and the bodies, she somehow made it to the back door, knowing it opened into the alley. She could get some air and it would all be okay.

Rough hands grabbed her by the shoulder and turned her around, taking her deeper into the building to the elevators. Moments later, she felt herself being escorted somewhere, her eyes unable to focus on the moving view as the exhilaration changed, transformed into the sharp edge of pain. She heard herself moan in the biting agony but it didn't relieve her, only elevated the pinching sensation under her skin.

Suddenly, she was horizontal, a bed beneath her back, and she blinked her eyes to see the ceiling.

Memories of watching ceilings on her back assaulted her; the black hole beckoned again. But she was too hot, her skin felt uncomfortable. Someone tore her clothes off, leaving her naked on the cool sheets. Lost between the pain and delirium that called to her, she needed something. She needed more. God, what did she need? Her body sweat as her heart raced overtime, thumping in her chest, each chest bringing her a second closer to a certain death. Was she going to die? Was this it?

"We live online?"

"Yeah."

A sharp pain in her nipple made her cry out as someone's mouth covered it.

"No!" she tried to push them away, struggling, and someone slapped her hard, making her head spin faster. But thankfully whoever it was left her alone.

"Upload the feed. He's going to come once he sees this."

Someone spoke, and she knew she needed to focus on the words to understand what was happening, but it felt slow like she was trying to walk through sludge. Where was she? What bed was this? Who was coming?

Him.

He was coming.

A wave of relief so acute swept over her she began to cry. But no, he couldn't come. They were waiting. They would get him, and she didn't want that. Who would make her feel safe then? Who would give her answers? Who would she trust? Did she trust him? No. Yes. A bit. Maybe. What was she thinking? Why was she so feverish?

Minutes or hours or nights passed she didn't know; she looked at the ceiling, writhing on the bed to find some semblance of comfort, her body burning as she breathed, her heart pounding in a way it was scaring her. She tried to inhale to calm down but couldn't focus enough, could focus on nothing.

All of a sudden, the ceiling disappeared, the room going pitch black.

She whimpered.

She didn't like the dark. Memories of being trapped in dark spaces came to her, her fear making her shiver as she began to sob. She was alone, and she was going to die, overdosed by a drug she didn't know, as bait for a man she didn't know, by strangers who didn't care. Nobody cared. What was even the point of living?

Something cold pressed against her cheek, making her seek more of the coolness that gave her a brief moment of respite.

A hand. Leather.

"Shh." The voice of death came from the darkness, his voice, right next to her ear. "I'm here, *flamma*. Shh."

A sharp cry of relief left her unbidden even as her mind revolted. No, no, he couldn't be here. She had to warn him. But she'd promised he wouldn't hear her voice again. But she didn't want him to die. Fuck the promise. He had to live.

"It . . .it's . . .a tr..trap," she stuttered somehow, her teeth chattering as her eyes tried to find him. She couldn't see a thing in the utter darkness, but she felt him—muscled, solid, *there.*

"Don't worry about it," he reassured her, his voice soft, soothing almost, the leather going to the other cheek.

She shook her head, unable to see him. Finding the hand on her face, she touched his leather glove, gripping his wrist, sobs bursting out of her chest. "T . . .they drugg . . .gged me."

"And they will pay."

The promise of retribution in those words, knowing he would follow through, calmed her down just a bit. He was there. She would be okay.

"The drug is fatal. I don't know the dosage they gave you, but I'm not willing to take the risk. You have two options," he told her quietly, his dark voice making her focus for a moment. "Either I work the drug out of your system while you're barely conscious or I make you unconscious and let it flush itself out. That is longer and riskier."

She didn't want to be there longer. She shook her head against his hand again, and he probably understood.

"The drug will make you delirious as the effects sharpen. You won't be fully conscious."

"I trust you," she managed to whimper as a bolt of heat ran through her body, making her spasm.

"That's exactly what sealed your fate all those years ago."

She knew that. She had trusted him with something important and he had never let her escape since.

The sensation of his gloved hands on her thighs made her gasp, the sensation heightened by whatever was in her system and the pitch black of the room. The lack of sight made her acutely aware of where his hands were, and how large they felt on her limbs.

She felt him push her legs open, heat arrowing to the juncture of her thighs but not wetness. She felt his shoulders, wide, wide shoulders, split and hold her open as his breath fell on her pussy. Breasts heaving, she clenched the sheets on her side as his mouth made contact with her there for the first time in their first kiss.

Wetness coated her as he flicked her clit with the tip of his tongue, before the flat of his tongue took over, the skill of his mouth making her gush in a way she'd never before, making her feel sensations so sharp it wasn't pleasurable, it was almost pain. She cried as he did it, the heaviness in her limbs increasing with each passing second.

And then, for the first time in years, she felt herself come immediately, quicker than she would've thought possible. Maybe it was the drug, maybe it was him, maybe it was a combination of both. She didn't know and didn't care. She just came, and it felt . . . incomplete. It felt painful, without an iota of pleasure.

But it took the edge off for a minute.

"Your trust, *flamma,* is the most addictive drug."

The quiet words penetrated her hazed mind as she looked down to where his voice was coming from, seeing nothing, almost like an invisible man was touching her. The Shadow Man. *Her* man.

"I won't give you more of it," she told him in her split second of clarity, and felt his teeth on the inside of her thigh.

"You will. Every atom in your body sings for me too."

His words reminded her of the note, her thighs clenching around his shoulders in recall. "My body's reactions mean nothing." With the way it had been used and abused over the years, she didn't trust it. She didn't even like it. The self-loathing phase she had for her body in the beginning was long gone; it was just numbness now.

Something warm pressed into her clit, making her gasp. "Even meaningless, they're all mine."

She wanted to refute his statement but another wave of haze came over her. She cried, sobbing because he claimed her without claiming her, he wanted her without wanting her, and she needed more, she needed him, and he didn't give her that. She cried and resisted as the pain in her body increased, and he stayed until she surrendered. His mouth wreaked havoc as he made her come again and again and again, to the point where she passed out, or she thought she did. A large part of it went blank for her, but her body kept responding, kept reacting, kept coming, leaving her sore and satiated yet empty and incomplete, clenching with a thirst she felt in her soul, never to be quenched.

Yet, he stayed with her.

CHAPTER 7

HIM

This accelerated things.

Orgasm after orgasm, sensory overload for him, changed everything.

Since his memory served, his sensory receptors hadn't worked right. He had never been able to respond to any sight or sound, even if he registered it. But seeing her had felt like finding the richest shades of his favorite colors, seared across his retinas with a taste of something sweet on his tongue. People had said that was an odd experience because of his eyes, but he knew it wasn't that. His perception of things was just different. But it was her voice that he couldn't explain. The first time he heard her speaking, the sound had sent vibrations over his skin, like a tuning fork hit with something, rippling across his body with such vividness it was unheard of, again leaving him with the sweet taste on his tongue. He had sought her out again, just to see for himself if it had been a fluke or real.

His body still buzzed from the vibrations of her words, her little cries, her strangled moans, his mouth filled with both her juices and the sensory sweet taste, a combination he was becoming addicted to with each passing second. It was real. And whatever it was, it was his. He didn't care if she had this effect on any other human. He would eradicate them all until he was the only one left standing, if that was the case.

Her exhausted body jerked in her slumber, and he ran a finger over her delectable mouth. Lush lips pillowed under his touch and he wondered what she would taste like there. He had never kissed someone on the mouth, never really had the urge to. Why would he want a stranger's mouth so close to his own and their fluids in his body? It made no sense. Fucking, he could understand. It was a biological need, but kissing wasn't. Oral wasn't either, which was one of the reasons he had never tasted pussy either. But he was well-versed in the ways of pleasure, and with her taste cemented on him, he doubted he'd taste another again, just hers.

He was going to be her last and she would be his first in so many ways.

He pressed the heel of his hand down on his cock, the piercings straining as it continued to throb, hard for the hours he'd been wringing out delicious orgasms from her pussy. His tongue, the same tongue her pussy had spasmed around through the night, was swollen with sensation.

Oh, he was going to fuck her, fuck her *hard.* He would take her like that one day, he decided. Maybe slide inside her while she slept, make her give him her trust to the point her body intuitively reacted to him even in her sleep. And in the morning, she would wake up sore with no memory of how but feeling him in every inch of her delicate, delicious cunt. He was going to test her trust, take every little ounce that she had in her capacity, until her body, her mind, her fucking *soul* believed in how important she was.

She was *it*.

She was *the* reason.

She saw him for who he was, and she melted for him. She hated him, and yet she trusted him. What had begun as intrigue had turned into fascination, slowly morphing into a fixation, culminating in an obsession so deep he was incomplete without it.

And one day very soon, she would be entirely his.

Not right now. Right now, the drug was bad enough to mess with her system. She didn't need him to add to it.

Covering her with the blanket in the hotel room above the club, a place he knew like the back of his hand thanks to his own past, he was on the move, able to see through the pitch black thanks to his night-vision glasses. The darkness was for her, to shield her from the cameras, their audios disabled. With the way the room was locked and darkened, no one would dare to come in, not unless they wanted to risk facing him.

And no one in this world in their right minds wanted to face the Shadow Man in the dark.

Touching her cheek with his gloved hand, his mouth and chin wet from her, her taste etched on his tongue and his memory, he let the neurons in his brain register the rush they were feeling.

She had spoken to him, to warn him, to save him. Despite all her anger and hurt, she cared for him. Soft-hearted little fool, but *his* fool. She was rare, the fire of life, of warmth. He didn't understand emotions, but he understood science. Something happened chemically in his brain and his body where she was concerned. He looked at her, heard her, and felt sensations in his system. It was the oddest response, one he had extensively researched, only to realize it was some form of synesthesia and it didn't have a rational explanation in all cases. The wires in his brain were simply crossed, and they simply electrified when crossed with hers, and that was something he knew already.

Leaving her in the aftermath of her intense drug-induced episode, he walked to the door and looked out the peephole. Three men with guns waiting for him, as expected. Idiots.

Taking steps back into the room, he checked the feed on his phone before pushing it into his pocket, and headed for the window. Wedging it open easily, he jumped on the ledge, the adrenaline rushing to his body at the height. He liked heights. It reminded him of the home he would take her to one day.

Holding the upper edges of the window, he jumped onto the pipe that ran on the side of the building, his trained muscles working with memory, and began to climb up, one foot on the window edges, another on the pipe, glad that he'd worn his athletic workout gear. That had been more incidental than deliberate though. He had seen the feed from her room coming online, and known within seconds it was a trap for him and she was the bait.

They didn't know she wasn't the bait he would bite, she was the prize he had already won in this bloody game—he just had to claim the winning.

But he realized a message, a louder message, needed to be sent.

Coming to a stop on the window five stories above where she was, he looked in and saw it occupied with Howard and two girls, both of them sucking on his cock as he lay in bed, grinning with the mouth he had put on *his girl.*

The other man was going to regret that.

With the stealth of a cat, years of martial arts and parkour training kicking in automatically, he swung himself to hang from one hand until his other got a solid grip on the windowsill. Holding himself steady, checking to see all occupants of the room were distracted, he slowly opened the window and jumped in noiselessly, immediately ducking behind a giant couch on one side.

"Blasted window," he heard Howard mutter. "Doll, go shut it."

He stayed still as one of the girls closed the window and turned back, just as a knock sounded on the door. Someone, he assumed the girl, opened it.

"What's the status?" Howard asked, the sound of sucking resuming.

"The room has been quiet for a few hours. Dark too. We don't have visual."

"You think he's come yet?"

"Doubt it. The entrances are monitored. We're on high alert."

Their security was laughable. He wondered if the Syndicate knew how terrible the operations were on ground level or if they even cared.

The noise of Howard's grunt came, followed by the rustling of the girls scrambling up and leaving.

"Keep an eye on her room. If he doesn't show up by dawn, kill the girl."

A burn began at the base of his spine at the words.

Any normal man would've felt anger perhaps, or even lust for revenge. He felt neither. In his head, it was a simple equation that had been messed with. Emotion didn't fit into that; it didn't need to. Was that psychotic? Maybe. But he had never pretended to be anything else than the devil he was.

A few minutes later, the door shut, and he heard the other man settling down in his bed, the lights going out.

Shadows formed over the room, and that's when he took over.

Straightening from his crouch, he walked on silent feet to the bed, watching the out-of-shape shirtless man slumbering. The man was a spineless coward on a power trip. Having the meeting with him at the housing complex alone had made him realize that.

He had visited the housing complex to see their security under the guise of a meeting as an investor looking to purchase assets. The complex had incredible security, one he would need to navigate if he had to get to her once they locked her in, and after this, they probably would. But she had to keep trusting him—he would find her and this time, he would take her out.

Something akin to excitement filled him at the thought.

Walking to the table, he checked the bottle of whiskey. 100 proof. *Good.*

Taking the bottle, he opened it and poured around the edges of the bed first, slowly emptying it. He then went to the cabinet, got another 100 proof bottle, and returned to the bed. Tipping it over, he poured some down on the sleeping man.

Howard jerked awake with a sputter, his eyes flying everywhere until they fell on his silhouette, terror taking over his face. They said you saw the Shadow Man before you died. And from the look on his face, Howard knew of the rumors.

"No, please, I'll give you whatever you want," he begged like the spineless swine he was, wetting the bed with fear, the stench of alcohol and urine mixing with the stink that his voice left in his nose. It was odd, how he smelled and tasted voices, none of them palatable except hers.

He looked down at the man, remembering the video footage he had pulled up from the club on his way, remembering the way Howard had touched her hair, *his* hair, and poured the drugged concoction down her throat, put his filthy mouth on her breast as she begged and cried for mercy.

The burn in his spine rippled into a blaze at the memory.

No, his message had to be clear to every single one of them.

Taking the other man's hair in his gloved fist, he pulled it hard, making the man cry out. "Please, no, let me go. I'll do whatever you want. Please."

"Drink," he threw the same word out that they had used with her. He hadn't been able to see the other man who had drugged her, one with the lighter hair, but he would find out. If there was one thing he was good at, it was at finding information.

Gulping, shaking, Howard opened his mouth.

Tipping the bottle, he poured the drink raw down the other man's throat until he spluttered and coughed. Finally, once the entire bottle was almost empty, he stepped back. A look of relief came over the other man's face, thinking that was it.

He let him think it.

Pouring the last of the alcohol in his mouth, he pulled at his hair. "Hold it."

The shaking man held the alcohol in his open mouth, his eyes wide with such sheer terror it made the Shadow Man calm. He dumped the empty bottle to the side and took his lighter from his pocket, flipping it up.

The other man begging in noises, he kept Howard's neck tilted completely back, and touched the flame in the lighter to the liquid in his mouth.

The fire took over, heating up the alcohol surrounding his tongue, the same tongue that had touched her. The man began to scream, struggling, but he held him immobile as the fire found its way into his throat just like the drug had gone down hers.

"Touch her and you die," he remarked quietly. "Touch her worse, die worse. It's a simple thing, isn't it? I don't know why you didn't understand it."

The other man was too gone in his pain to focus so he stepped back, walking to the door, seeing Howard trying to get off the bed toward the bathroom. Before he could set his foot down, the Shadow Man took flipped the lighter again, the lighter with the snake insignia of The Syndicate—an ouroboros, to be precise—and threw it on the bed, watching in satisfaction as flames erupted on the soaking sheets, spreading to the boundary of the bed, burning the man alive inside and out, his screams grating on his senses.

He left his lighter behind so the message was clear to everyone in the system—he knew their symbol, he knew who they were, and he would not hesitate in doing to them what he'd done here. She was *off-limits.*

This time, he left through the main door, keeping away from the cameras, taking the fire exit stairs out of the building.

Things had changed.

He needed to finish his final mission before he took her home. He needed to get her home, get her trust and her loyalty before he opened the door to her past.

But that was later. He was leaving breadcrumbs to figure things out, and that brought him enough time.

For now, she'd be safe, she'd be unharmed, and he could live with that.

CHAPTER 8

LYLA

Waking up with her head and her body feeling like it was weighed down by a ton of bricks, Lyla blinked her eyes open to see a familiar ceiling over her head. The medical room at the complex. What was she doing there?

Light filtered in through a small window, but she couldn't move her limbs to get up from the soft bed. It felt wonderful to simply lie and soak up the comfort, as her mind tried to recall the last thing it could remember.

Drugged. She'd been drugged.

A dark room. Cameras. Heat. *Him.*

Him between her thighs, devouring her over and over until she lost consciousness. She didn't know how long he ate her out after that. The idea sent an odd shiver of thrill down her spine—the idea that she had been completely at his mercy to do as he pleased. The thought, with anyone else, filled her with terror and disgust. And yet, closing her eyes and imagining her invisible lover in the dark, she couldn't completely throw the thought out.

She was an idiot, that's what she was. A fucking idiot for trusting the most dangerous man she could find, who played with her, had no allegiance to anyone or anything whatsoever. And yet, he had showed up every time she had needed him. And though it had been a trap for him, he had come for her again.

What game was he playing?

Frustrated at herself for letting the question circle her mind, she tried to sit up, struggling under the heaviness of the lingering effects of the drug.

The door opened. Three entered the room with one of the girls she didn't know but had seen in the building. The contempt on the woman's face made her stomach drop. She looked at them both, trying to understand what had happened.

"I don't understand what's so special about you," the older woman remarked, her lips curving in a sneer. "He has been lining the street with bodies in your wake."

Three indicated for the younger girl to set a tray of food on the table beside her as she kept talking. "I don't know what you got yourself into last night, but he killed Mr. H because of it."

Lyla felt her breath hitch. "What?"

The older woman shook her head. "Yes, foolish girl. Mr. H died because of you. Do you know how good he was to the girls? How generous? Thanks to you, Set him on fire alive."

Lyla stayed silent.

"Congratulations, the higher ups are going to watch you like a hawk now."

A sliver of anger rippled through her.

How the fuck was any of that her fault? Mr. H hadn't been a

divine pagan of virtue. He had drugged her and touched her and she wasn't sorry he died. She wasn't sorry any of them died. But once again, someone else's actions had impacted her life, and she just didn't want to deal with it. But living in the world she did, trapped as she was, what choice did she have?

Three poured her a glass of juice and pointed to the food. "Rest for a few days, and then get packed. Orders. You have a new ... assignment. You're moving."

Biting her lip, Lyla swerved her eyes from the girl at the door, back to Three. She knew better than to ask about her new station. She would find out when she was escorted to wherever she was going.

"Any news on Malini?" she asked her handler for the last time, knowing she would know or at least have some inkling of where the girl could be. If she was moving, she needed to ask for one final time.

The older woman's eyes chilled. "She's been contracted. I won't tell you again."

But it was odd for someone under contract to not come back for any of their stuff at all. Possessions, as meagre as they were, were important to every girl in there. She knew that. They were things they had collected over the years, little trinkets of comfort that mattered to them because nothing else did. All girls who were contracted were given a last trip to pack their stuff and say goodbye. But not Malini. She had woken up one morning, gone to work at an online auction, and never returned. While it was entirely possible that whoever had bought her hadn't allowed her any time to return, something inside Lyla couldn't shake off the feeling that it wasn't that. Something else had happened to the other girl.

Keeping her thoughts to herself, she drank the juice and ate the toasted bread as Three left. The girl, a blondish, petite beauty, hesitated in the doorway, her eyes going to where their handler was disappearing.

"I don't know where they're sending you, but it's not good," the girl whispered urgently. "Just . . . be prepared."

With that, the girl rushed out too, leaving her alone with her thoughts, a maelstrom in her mind. They were sending her . . . somewhere not good.

She didn't know what was coming, but she didn't know if she was prepared for it.

For the next few days, Lyla rested and let her body recover from the aftermath of whatever drug she had been forced to consume. She was given a few days off work, so she just rested and wandered in the house, eavesdropping on different conversations. That was how she stopped outside the kitchen, listening to the chatter inside.

"What do you think the deal is with the Shadow Man and Lyla?" someone asked.

Lyla pressed into the wall, curious to know what others were thinking about the whole thing.

"I didn't even think he was real until all this. Now, I'm not sure what to think."

"I think he's just a client gone territorial," another voice chimed in.

"Lyla hasn't had a client since she came here," a girl pointed out. "He takes them out."

"Maybe he loves her."

Lyla gripped her shorts, her heart racing. He wasn't capable of loving, and she wasn't desperate enough yet to imagine he could.

Two girls laughed inside, the sound chipping into her. "That doesn't exist here, Millie. Maybe he just wants to get her out."

"But why hasn't he already then? It's been like . . . what six years?"

Ouch. That hurt.

"I think he's just using her for his own agenda, whatever it is. That's all we're good for anyway."

Listening to the conversation, a large part of her agreed.

He had some agenda, and she was just what she'd always been—collateral with damage.

A week after the drug incident, she was thrown out of the complex figuratively, and her nerves were fraught. Not only because she was moving again and the girl's warning was ringing in her head, but because he had been absent. She hadn't seen him since the incident, or even felt him, and the absence was gnawing, spinning her mind, making her thoughts oscillate between him having an agenda and him genuinely caring for her in his own twisted way. The more the time passed without him, the more the latter thought flickered.

In record time, she packed her entire collection of material possessions in one box, and waited outside the building as one of the guards came to collect her. He put a blindfold over her eyes, routine if they were being transferred to some secure location, and it disoriented her, not knowing where she was going.

She knew it was the fallout from that night, she knew it had something to do with Mr. H's death and whatever message it sent. She just didn't know if it was good for her or not. The guard deposited her in a vehicle and she heard thc ignition start, driving away from the longest housing period she had been in. She had been seventeen when she had come to this Complex, eighteen when she'd met *him* for the first time, eighteen when her life had changed on one fateful night.

With the blackness behind the blindfold, she could remember the thunder and the raindrops splattering her as she'd run into the woods around the complex, desperately seeking escape when she'd collided—

The car jerked, breaking her thoughts, splintering them until she took a deep breath and centered herself. Memories, her memories, were a powerful vortex that sucked her in every time, taking her to dark places. She couldn't remember a single moment in her life where she felt happy without the pressing weight of something terrible. She didn't know how to smile anymore, the lines between her eyebrows becoming more permanent than they were not.

"Who are we going to?" she asked, just to break the monotony of her thoughts, not really expecting a reply.

"Don't know," the guard told her. "I'm just the delivery guy."

Nice.

The car came to a stop after a long time. She heard the guard opening his door, before coming to her side, and hauling her out. She felt the sun on her skin for a split second before he guided her up some low steps. Still blindfolded, she stumbled her way through, her only box of possessions clutched against her chest. He took her down a long walkway, the ground under her flats solid, like concrete of some kind. Musky scents assaulted her nostrils, too mixed up together for her to discern.

Finally, after what felt like hours of walking, she was pushed into a chair.

The blindfold was taken off, and she blinked rapidly to let her eyes adjust to the sudden light, realizing she was in some kind of warehouse office, in a room made of wood, one with a brown table that was so rough and scratched it was probably older than she was, and—she counted—four chairs around it.

Wondering what this new place was and what her role in it was going to be, she took it in, waiting.

And waiting.

And waiting.

After a long time, a door opened and three men, dressed in jeans and t-shirts, walked in. Nervous energy filled her, her feet tapping the ground as she looked at the three strange men, not knowing who they were. But they looked menacing, rough, one of them even more so. The mean one was bald, his head gleaming as he took a seat at the head of the table, wearing a ring with the same snake design as the man from the club that night.

The other two deferred to him, coming to stand in front of her chair.

"You've cost my bosses a lot of money and a lot of men, Lyla," the mean one, the leader clearly, spoke. "What should we do with you?"

She stayed silent, her heart pounding, a sense of dread infiltrating her veins as she looked at the men.

"You're too important to let go of, but too useless to the business. You were leverage against some powerful people, and now you're also leverage against the Shadow Man." The eagerness of the man's voice scared her. "Do you know who he is?"

She shook her head quickly. She genuinely didn't know who he was.

The man studied her for a long minute. "The Shadow Man came out of nowhere about ten years ago. He became a legend in the underworld. Disrupted our path again and again, and to this day I don't understand what his end-goal is. So, let me rephrase. Do you know *anything* about him?"

She shook her head again.

"You wouldn't be lying now, would you?"

She wasn't lying.

"Good," he smiled, his face creasing in laugh lines that should have made him look nice. "We have traveled a long way to see you. Why don't you get on your knees and make us feel better?"

Swallowing, she looked at each of them, finding some semblance of strength inside her. "That would be signing your death warrant. He kills everyone."

One of the men stepped closer, suffocating her space. "We'll risk it. If he cares about you, maybe he'll find us. If not, it's our gain."

Grabbing her by the arm, he dragged her to the bald man.

Lyla looked around the room, knowing she was trapped, knowing there was no escape, feeling claustrophobic because day after day, there had been no reprieve. And this time, she knew in her gut he wasn't even aware of what was happening.

The man with her arm pushed her to her knees, the other took out his camera.

"Make the feed live," the bald man instructed from his place at the head of the table. "Let him see how we break his little toy."

Lyla closed her eyes.

No.

He wasn't there to save her, not like he'd told her, showed her, promised her he would be. And she couldn't save herself. He had lured her into a false sense of safety until she started relying on him, and now she was trapped because he had endangered her.

He had lied.

And *he* may kill everyone he wanted afterward, but it wouldn't be for her. It would be for himself, and it would never bring back the last piece of her that broke.

She closed her eyes, and let the black hole swallow her whole.

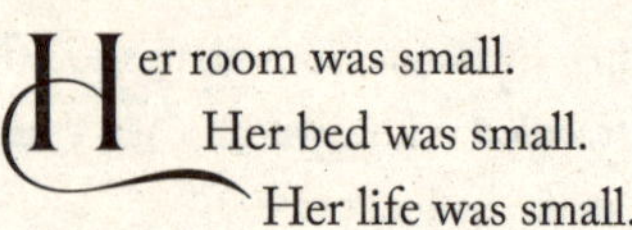

Her room was small.

Her bed was small.

Her life was small.

And it didn't matter.

She didn't matter, nothing mattered.

She was the black hole and the black hole was her, endless nothingness with no capacity for light.

She didn't know who came to her room, who left, who did what to her.

She felt nothing; she spoke nothing; she saw nothing.

She just stared at the cracked ceiling, recognizing the cracks within herself, widening, sharpening, lengthening.

Purposeless.

Endless.

Lifeless.

Days passed.

The ceiling stayed the same.

Months passed.

The ceiling got worse.

Time became meaningless.

The last sign of life in her body came when her box fell over, black roses scattering across the floor, sparking something.

She flew across the room in a rage and tore them apart, crushing the petals, bruising them until her eyes began to burn and her throat locked tight.

She wanted *nothing* of him. No reminders. Nothing of the man who had made her believe in an illusion of safety, only to push her into danger himself. He had betrayed her, time and time again, leaving her behind for the jackals to feed off her flesh.

Standing up, she went to the bathroom and grabbed a razor from the cabinet behind the mirror. Looking at herself, at her sunken eyes and her pallid reflection, at the hair he had been so fascinated with, she began to hack away at the long tresses she had never cut before. With each lock of hair that fell, she felt herself go, felt who she had been disappear as a silent doll took its place—good to use and play with, pretty to look at, but completely lifeless.

Cutting the last lock of her hair, she let him go, let herself go, let everything that connected them go.

The ceiling cracked.

PART 2

EMBERS

"Each time you happen to me all over again."

—Edith Wharton, *The Age of Innocence*

CHAPTER 9

LYLA | 6 MONTHS LATER

She was going to do it tonight.

She was going to end it.

It had taken her months to decide how, and she finally had a way that wouldn't hurt much.

A song played in the back, the beats loud. She didn't know the song, just moved her body in time with the beat on the stage, the leather chafing against her skin but still unable to wake her from her slumber. That's how she felt, like she was sleeping, going through the motions, and one day, she would simply wake up and all of it would be a bad dream.

For months, she had been like that. Months of being confined to a room until her captors had realized she was useless, that whatever lure they believed she held she didn't. She wasn't leverage, just dead weight, and they finally relocated her again. Now, she danced on the stage at a club she didn't know, and lived in one of the rooms above the the building alone.

But something had changed.

She was scared of being near people now.

Now, after being confined in one small, dark room for so long with nothing but herself, she was scared of being around people. Just being in the club had her sweating and shaking too much. Dancing was only possible if she closed her eyes and made herself believe she was alone. Song after song changed. People cheered and jeered from below, making her open her eyes, but she saw no one, just moving on autopilot, looking at the neon sign above the main door, focusing on it.

'Where the demons come to play.'

She didn't disagree with that. Demons, every single one of them. And she was finally going to escape from this hell.

Her shift passed without incident, only her feet hurting, reminding her she was still in her body. A sheen of sweat marred her face, a face that looked haunted, the choppy haircut she had given it so many weeks ago making it more so. She hated her hair, her skin, her flesh, every single part of herself. Sometime in between, her indifference toward her body had shifted again into loathing. She had thought of cutting herself, but somehow, the pain still had the power to scare her.

Shaking off her thoughts, she got down from the stage at the end of her shift and headed to the backroom, breathing through her mouth to not let all the people around her overwhelm her, focusing on where her locker was with her change of clothes. She had something else there too.

Thankfully, without incident, she reached, opening the locker after she checked that the coast was clear. She looked at the small sachets of blue powder she had stolen from some of the tables over a few days. Four packets. The first time they had drugged her, they had used only one. She was going to use all of them and make herself high while her heart gave out.

A twinge of guilt moved through her, for the one soul she would leave behind, but she shook her head. She was not worth knowing. It was for the best.

Pocketing the bags, she shut the locker and moved through the sidelines of the lounge area, toward the fire exit that led up to the rooms.

She avoided looking at anyone, but glanced up occasionally to check if her path was clear.

"Hey, Lyla!"

Body freezing, she turned to see one of the servers hand her a tray full of drinks.

"Mindy sprained her ankle. Take this up to Table 4 in the VIP area."

Fuck. Okay, she could do this.

Giving a nod, she balanced the tray in clammy hands and headed to the special section cordoned off for special guests, focusing on one step at a time, the sachets burning a hole in her shorts.

This club was more elite than all the others she'd been in, so it had a larger clientele that was top of the crème. Climbing the low steps lit by neon lights, she walked over to the fourth table from the back, her steps coming to a halt as she took in the group of men and women sitting at the table—three couples and one man, and not one of them looking like they fit in this part of the world. Well, no one except the giant man with an eye patch. He looked like he'd fit right in.

"You don't get it!" one of the women, a brunette with glasses, exclaimed loudly, glaring at the man beside her who was looking down at the tablet she was showing him. "How can you not see this?"

Another woman, a beautiful modelesque stunner, just looked at them with visible amusement, sitting in the crook of an arm belonging to a well-dressed man in a suit. "Even I didn't the first time. Not everyone has your eye for detail, Morana."

Such a pretty name.

The eye-patch man sat opposite them, a woman with blue hair close to his side. "He sent it to me last week. He's been after Hector harder than we have."

"I wonder why," the brunette with glasses mused out. "It's the first time I'm sensing some kind of stakes in this for him."

It was such an odd dynamic, one she had never seen before but immediately recognized. She felt a hollow pang go through her chest. *Friends. Family.* They looked like family together.

Silently putting the drinks on the table, skilled at going unnoticed, she moved around the table, keeping her head down.

"Thank you," the beautiful woman said softly to her, but Lyla didn't look up. Throat tight, she turned to leave, taking the kind word back with her, the image sticking in her mind of the group of friends sharing camaraderie. In another life, she could've been a girl with a group of friends enjoying drinks on a night. In another life, she could've been a woman tucked under the arm of a man who clearly cared for her. In another life. Maybe, if she had a next one, it would be kinder to her.

She rounded the corner of the VIP area, and out of their line of sight, turned around, glancing at them again.

It was a nice thing to see on the last night of her life.

Carrying the levity of witnessing their interactions in her heart, she dumped the tray on the counter and finally headed to her room, climbing the fire exit stairs to the first floor, her room the last on the landing.

Turning the knob, she entered and shut the door behind her,

heading straight to the only furniture in the room—her tiny bed. It was so small that a taller woman would have a hard time sleeping on it straight.

Taking the packets of blue powder from her shorts, she placed them in her lap, staring at them. A bottle of water sat on the floor by her leg, and she uncapped it. Ripping the packet open, she dumped all the four sachets into the water and gave it a good shake with trembling hands.

Heart pounding, hands shaking worse with each second, she stared at the liquid.

This was it.

This was how it ended.

Taking a deep breath, she brought the bottle to her lips. And she tipped it up.

The bitter liquid went down her throat as she gulped, taking in as much as she could before her stomach felt full.

Bottle empty, she put it down and lay down on the bed, staring at the ceiling.

It was a nice ceiling, with fake ornamental designs around the fan, making it look pretty. Not like the many cracked, peeling ceilings she had looked at. It was a nice last ceiling. Why was she thinking of ceilings?

Tears streamed down the side of her face as she lay alone in the dark, the light from a street lamp outside casting shadows in the room, reminding her of *him*.

She let herself think of him for the first time in months. A nameless man who had changed her life for both the better, at least for a while, and then worse. A nameless man who had made her believe, in his own twisted way, that she was worth something, that her life mattered to someone, that she was cared for.

Was that why her heart bled so much? Because he had abandoned her, left her lost and adrift like everything else? Because he had made her care too, and she had paid the price for it? Because in all the months since he had not once come seeking her?

'I'll always come for you.'

Liar.

Had he found a new obsession, a new girl to kill for? Or had he simply gotten bored with their games once he had a taste of her? Had it been that, the fact that he'd had her in some way, the thrill of the chase gone?

For a moment, she wondered if it was because he was dead or injured, but knowing him, she couldn't believe it for more than a second. The intensity of his obsession at its peak had made her believe he would have crawled to find her if he she were out of his sight. No, he was alive, and she was abandoned.

The first wave of heat hit her body, her skin beginning to pinch and tighten.

She closed her eyes, holding the sides of the bed and wave after wave of heat spiked to a fever in her system, her heart thumping so rapidly and loudly in her chest she couldn't hear anything but the pounding in her ears.

The pounding came insistently, jolting her, her eyes flying to the door.

Someone was actually pounding on her door. *What the hell?*

"Hey Lyla, you got some concealer? This guy bruised me bad."

It was one of the other girls on the landing. Lyla stayed still, deciding to ignore her. It wasn't like she could get up anyway if she tried. It felt nice, just lying there as her body collapsed on itself.

The pounding faded away, the only noise in her ears of a whoosh, maybe her own blood. Her eyelids began to feel heavy, so she closed them, feeling like the earth was shaking underneath her.

No, it was shaking.

She was shaking.

Something was shaking her.

"Look at me!"

The loud, sharp command made her eyelids peel open to a slit, immediately locking with the devil's gaze.

Death had come to take her, after all.

She smiled.

"Take me gently, death. I've been waiting for you," she whispered, her mind dizzy, her eyes closing again.

"Open your eyes, flamma."

A low, guttural demand followed by a touch on her cheek had her eyes opening again. He checked her eyes, put his hand on her neck, then growled, *"Fuck!"*

She felt something pinch at the side of her neck but wrote it off. She had been thinking of him, and in her last moments, her brain was being kind to her. That was a saving grace. Her delusions were taking pity on her. She couldn't really complain.

"You." Her voice was barely audible, her body slumping as he picked her up in his arms. "Tell me . . . tell me where he is . . ."

"Live for me and I'll tell you," he bargained as always, tucking her body close to his torso. He was cold and warm at the same time, and so, so solid. She wished she'd had him to hold on so many nights.

Tears fell down her face, and she tucked her nose in his neck, breathing in his distinctive scent.

"Please. It's my last wish," she cried softly, and felt his arms tighten around her. The delusion-him was nice too, he almost made her believe he was concerned for her.

"You have many wishes left in you, *flamma,* and I will lay every single one of them at your feet. Just keep fucking *breathing*, got that?"

The dark, guttural notes of his voice hit her simultaneously with another wave of heat. She whimpered and buried herself closer to him, grateful to her mind for conjuring him up so she wouldn't feel alone in her last moments.

They were moving at a rapid pace. Noises and sights blurred, and she felt her limbs get heavier and heavier, her heart suddenly slowing, making her head spin.

"Were you . . . with someone else?" she asked on a hiccup, voicing her worst fear, her fingers tightening over his jacket as he lay her down somewhere, strapping her with belts. What was her mind doing? Why was it making him strap her somewhere?

He finished pulling the belts tight so she couldn't move and gripped her face, making her focus for one second on his devilish mismatched eyes.

"You have been, you are, and you will always be my only obsession, Luna Caine."

She cried out at the fact that he took another girl's name, a sharp pain piercing her heart, before everything went black.

CHAPTER 10

HIM

T*oo fucking close.*

He had almost lost her, and for the first time in his memory, something *livid* lay breathing in his chest. Emotions weren't something he felt, but he was *feeling.* Mainly, at himself for not finding her sooner, for taking so long to wrap up loose ends. Also at her, for thinking he would let her go, for even contemplating that she could and he wouldn't bring her back from the jaws of death itself. It couldn't have her, *nothing* could have her, until he released his claim.

If their past had taught them anything, it was that time meant nothing in their relationship. He would wait years for the right time with her, but the fact that she hadn't had the patience told him two very important things—she was broken more than he had estimated, and he needed to do whatever it took to make her alive again. If she didn't feel again, the world would cease to be.

Her life wasn't hers to take.

He looked at where he'd strapped her in the chopper, flying over the city and the fields to the east, taking her where she should have always been.

She moaned in pain, the sound clear in his earpiece through hers, and the vibrations of the sound rippled down his forearms, the sweet aftertaste filling his mouth.

He had missed that. He'd missed *her.* And he'd almost lost her. That wasn't okay. That wasn't in the *vicinity* of okay.

As he flew over the dark fields below, he realized what a close call tonight had been—in more ways than one. Tristan Caine had been there, too close, with the rest of his people, and *he* wasn't ready for her to go yet. He knew what would happen if she was gone too early. She would find her family, find people who loved her endlessly, find a man who would heal her with love, probably that dog of Dante's who'd been on her scent for months, or maybe someone else. And maybe they would quieten her demons for a while. But the demons would return. None of them would understand that, understand her, her hell, because none of them had even seen it, much less lived through it. She needed to feel safe to heal, and no one would make her feel safer than he would. Because they had conscience, morals, ethics, and he? He had her.

She could never be anyone else's. She'd been claimed by a devil in the shadows long before anyone could bring her to light.

And even surrounded by all the love, she would find herself feeling isolated, alone, and wondering if she was too broken to be okay. And he wasn't okay with that. He had known for a while she had a disposition for self harm, mostly in her thoughts. She hadn't acted on it as far as he knew before tonight. That had been one of the reasons he'd always dangled the one thing he knew she wanted more than anything—her answers—in front of her as incentives for living, and it had worked for a while. He had to give her something to live for again.

She wasn't ready to meet her past yet, her mind probably wouldn't be able to handle it all at once, but one day she would be. And that day, he would lay the truth at her feet.

Handling the chopper easily with years of flying experience, he turned right toward the mountains that lined the land before the sea gaped open, heading to the home he had built for them over the years. Flying was one of the only things, beside playing with fire and stalking her, that he enjoyed.

"Am I dead?" the object of his obsession muttered, and he looked back at her, to see her blinking before she passed out again, her short hair sticking out around her beautiful face.

He knew why she'd cut it off, just like he knew why she'd ripped his roses. In her conscious mind, a part of her hated him. But her heart was soft, and it was starved for him, and he would do whatever it took to make her feel for him again.

After what she'd been through at the hands of The Syndicate, after what they'd done just to draw him out, he didn't blame her for her hatred. But he couldn't have come out even if he could have found her. It would have unraveled years of careful planning and putting the right pieces in the right spot. One impulsive move from him could have undone it all and gotten everyone, including the family she didn't even know about, killed.

No, he'd had to choose, and he hadn't chosen her in the short-term, but she had always been his choice. Everything he'd done for the last six years had been for her, so she could live one day freely without looking over her shoulder all the time.

And after what they had done, The Syndicate was going to *fucking burn.*

CHAPTER 11

LYLA

It was becoming A bad habit waking up in strange beds and looking at strange ceilings. Lyla blinked her eyes open, her limbs too weighed down for her to even try to move.

It took her a second to realize there was an *actual* weight on her, holding her down.

Panicking, she looked down at the bare muscular biceps resting on her stomach, down to the ripped forearm dusted with dark hair going diagonally to her hip, to the large, masculine hand holding her with long, tapered fingers. Burn marks littered places on the back of the hand.

Lyla moved her eyes up to see the man the arm was attached to and found herself ensnared by mismatched devilish eyes, one black, one golden-green, staring at her quietly.

It had been real.

Her fever dream had been real.

He had come for her, albeit after months, but he had.

Facts registered simultaneously in her brain—he was shirtless but she was dressed in something soft, his body was pressed to her side and his face close to her pillow, and there was a lot of natural gray light coming in from somewhere.

Ignoring the first two facts and ignoring him, she turned her neck to seek the source of the light.

And she stopped breathing.

The largest sets of windows she had ever seen showed something she had only ever seen pictures of. Mountains. Tall, majestic, gray mountains.

Scrambling from the bed and pushing his arm away, she tried to stand just as her knees buckled. She almost went down before strong arms effortlessly swung her up in an embrace she recalled from her delirium.

"Easy," he told her softly, but she ignored him, focused on the vista bare before her.

He carried her toward the glass, toward what she now realized was a set of double doors and not windows. Pushing it open with his foot, he walked them out. A blast of cold air assaulted her skin, making her instinctively curl closer to his body heat, the silk sleep shorts he must have put her in too thin to stand the weather.

He walked them to the edge and placed her on her feet, imprisoning her from the back with both arms on the metal railing, his presence behind her warm in the cold.

But she was focused on the view, on the feeling of being outside.

Her eyes greedily gulped the sight before her, unable to understand how places like this could even exist as she took in every inch of it.

Tall, beautiful, rocky gray mountains spanned as far as the eyes could see on her right, the view wrapping around until it disappeared on the side. On the other side to the left, a gray sea churned under the clouds endlessly, waves after waves crashing on the rocky beach in the distance, a beach created by the natural slope and decline of the mountains that went into the water. And right below her, the cliff steeped into a long, narrow body of water that joined the sea.

It was exquisite, surreal, unbelievable.

"What is this place?" she whispered in awe, unable to believe her own eyes.

"It's called Bayfjord," he informed her from her back. "That's the Iron Mountains, and that's the Black Bay."

She took in the sight for a long time, standing in the cage of his arms, unable to register it all, register that not only was she alive, she was in heaven and she was with him.

Reluctantly, she turned around so she could see the house they were in. A gasp left her as she stared up at the rough gray rocks.

They were on some kind of deck made in a slit of the space within the mountain. *Within* the mountain.

"Are we . . .how . . . in the mountain?"

Her broken words made him take a step back, leaving her alone on the edge, and she clung to his hand, terrified of the steep fall off the cliff. And that was so contrary to the woman who had decided to end herself.

She saw him look down at their hands together, his large, dark, burned hands encompassing her small, soft, pale ones.

"Come with me." He tugged her forward, and she half-heartedly followed, not ready to go back into her own mind or how she felt about him right that second. There was something new to experience, something *good,* and she grabbed it with both hands.

He took her back to the warm bedroom inside, closing the glass doors. She took the time to look around and take in everything. It was the largest bedroom she had ever seen—everything within it big and classy. From where she stood near the deck doors, the biggest bed, made of black wood with the same colored headboard and side tables was on the right.

Leading the way, he pointed to the wide dark doors opposite the deck doors. "This is a walk-in closet."

He slid the door open, and Lyla stared in awe at the spacious room, lined on both sides with clothes. The right side had all masculine attire, rows of shirts and suits and jackets, all in blacks and grays and whites. The left was feminine, rows of dresses, tops, tees, in mostly whites and blacks, with an occasional color thrown in.

A sharp stab of something pierced through her chest at the sight.

Someone lived with him, shared a closet with him, and yet he stood there holding her hand. She scrunched her eyes close. She had no right to feel anything. That was how things worked in their world. He could have a gazillion women on call and still take her, and she couldn't deny him.

That didn't mean she wasn't feeling—

"We can add more color to your side if you like."

—wait what?

She pressed brakes on her rampant thoughts and took in the wardrobe again. That was for *her? What the hell?*

Oblivious to her thoughts, or maybe not, he let go of her hand and walked to the large mirror opposite the entrance.

"Come."

Curious, she walked to him, realizing her feet were bare and the carpet under her toes was *soft.* Coming to a stop at his side, she was startled when he pulled her into his back by her hips, looking at their reflections. She looked so much smaller compared to him, the top of her head coming barely to his chin, her frame slender where his was wide. He wasn't overly muscled but muscled enough to be both strong and sleek.

"Tell me what you see."

Frowning at the odd request, because she could clearly see their reflections, she shook her head. Her hair, almost shoulder length now, was sticking out around her face. Her eyes were exhausted and her shoulders drooped. He, on the other hand, looked sharp, dangerous, lethal, the shirtless torso and black sweatpants not taking away from his aura, exactly as he had always looked.

"What do you see?" he prodded again.

Lyla saw herself blink in the reflection. "You behind me."

She startled as he leaned in, his reflection joining hers closer, his face beside hers. "Exactly. I'm always behind you, even when you cannot see."

Her throat closed up, the black hole she had escaped into ever-present inside her, reminding her of the months leading up to the moment she had decided to give up. Just because he had somehow decided to come back and found her didn't absolve him of anything. He had betrayed her, and that wasn't something she could let go of.

Gritting her teeth, seeing her bright green eyes flashing in the reflection, she addressed him. "Were you behind me when they were raping my body?"

His grip on her hips tightened. His face remained neutral. "Yes."

A bitter laugh burst out of her. "That's even worse. Because that means you did nothing to stop it. And that means you don't care." Her eyes locked with his. "So you can take your fancy house and fancy clothes and fancy views, and get the fuck away from me. I don't need anything from you, not anymore."

His eyes blazed for a split second before she shrugged his grip off, and he let her.

Exiting the closet space, she blindly headed toward the door she assumed led outside the room, needing to get away from him, to distract herself, to do absolutely anything but deal with him. She just didn't have the energy anymore.

Pulling open the black door, she walked out onto a small cavernous landing, a couple of low steps leading up into a massive, and she meant *massive*, open space. The first thing she noticed was the high ceiling, normal ceiling and not rock-cut like on the deck. Was this not a part of the mountain?

She entered the huge open space, a sense of wonder filling her at the multiple windows and natural light filling in.

She had never seen anything like this in her life, never thought she would see something like this.

From where she stood on top of the bedroom landing, she could see a short corridor going to her right, to what looked like another bedroom of sorts from her vantage. Ignoring that, she took a few steps into the open space, turning around on the spot to take it all in. A large open kitchen to her right, separated from the main living room by tall island counters and a dining table for six people. To her left corner, a seating area with black couches and wooden table on the left corner, right by a set of windows, in front of the biggest television screen.

She stared at the screen, unable to remember the last time she'd seen a movie. There had been a small TV in the common room at the complex, but she had barely ventured down to watch it. Mostly, the girls had fought between themselves to decide on one thing, and Lyla had never been confrontational. She simply sat back and bit her tongue, going with the flow, keeping her head down, surviving. That was how she'd understood survival worked best—go unnoticed, go safe.

'How'd that work out for you?' a voice taunted in her head.

Taking in a shaky breath, she looked to the other corner of the room, toward another corridor going somewhere. On slow steps, she went to investigate, crossing the length of the space and admiring the view outside the windows. She just didn't understand how this portion of the house looked normal but the deck had been under the mountain. How was it built exactly?

Sidelining the question for the moment, she entered the corridor and went down the short space, curious to see what she would find on the other side of the large door she could see at the end. With a click of the lock, the knob turned in her hand and she pushed it open, freezing on the threshold.

A room—no, a long hall—with windows on the wall opposite the door, lit up the space filled with things. So many things. Books on shelves lined one end of the hall. A solid wooden desk with a chair and multiple computers sat on the other end. In between, the area was littered with a canvas on an easel, a box of shiny crystals and shiny metal wires, so many things her brain couldn't compute what they all were for.

"There's something for you here."

The voice came from her back, from a space away. She turned to see him standing, still shirtless, his muscular upper body exposed for her eyes, an expanse of honey brown skin and solid muscles and a smattering of dark hair. He stood with his hands in his sweatpants pockets, simply observing her observing things.

"There's a white tablet on the table. That's for you. You can spend your time in here deciding what you like," he continued when she didn't say anything. "Reading, painting, jewelry-making, watching TV, playing video games, doing things online—try everything and see what you enjoy. There's also a little garden outside if you want to give it a shot, but you'll have to wait a month or two for the weather to turn warmer. If you like nothing, we'll add more options. It's all yours."

Throat tight, she stared at him, everything crashing on her, unable to understand how he'd known something she'd always wanted, a chance to explore what she liked for herself, control of the television remote, the *outside*.

"How . . . how did you know?" she stuttered, because there was nothing she had ever verbalized or expressed to anyone, innocuous and intense little things.

He moved forward then, stepping into her personal space, slowly, lazily almost, but sleek, his devilish eyes pinning her in place. One of his hands came up, holding her jaw like he always did, just as his thumb brushed over her lips. Her lips parted at the soft, almost tender touch, not used to feeling any sensation at all for months. He dipped his thumb in, just a little, and she stayed still, her heart pounding but not sucking on it, not responding at all. He took his thumb out, painting her lips with her own wetness, leaving them glistening, his eyes moving to her mouth, the pupil in the light eye expanding. She watched it, fascinated.

"I know you, *flamma,*" he reminded her. "The deepest desires of your heart, the softest secrets of your soul, the meanest moments in your mind. I know them all, I own them. Every desire, every secret, every thought."

She couldn't deny that. And yet, the bitterness didn't abate.

"And I fit into your agenda of whatever you've been doing, isn't it? I'm useful to you. That's why you came for me. That's why I'm here."

He said nothing, just gazed at her steadily, and she didn't know if that was an affirmation or a denial.

She never knew with him.

It began to dawn on her, standing there in the doorway of his expensive house, locked in place by his firm grip on her face. She had just traded one kind of prison for another, a more dangerous kind, because she knew she was weak when it came to him, and though she was already broken beyond repair, he had the power to break her still.

CHAPTER 12

LYLA

She retreated into the bedroom after her short tour, locking the door behind her, and went to bed to sleep. She was still groggy, tired, her body drained and her mind at capacity to deal with all the rapid changes. She had never been good with changes, always questioning things, questioning herself and her self-worth, whatever little of it she had.

And she needed space away from . . . *everything.* She needed the space to process her new state of being, process what she'd tried to do, process all the emotions seeing him again had roused within her. She needed . . . she didn't know what she needed. Tears welled up in her eyes as she stared at the view through the window, at both the fact that he had given her this and the fact that she still didn't matter beyond whatever her usefulness to him was.

She was vulnerable in every way to him, and it burned in her chest to realize it.

She looked out at the mountains, wondering if she had the courage to actually jump off the cliff to escape. Stealing the drugs and drinking that mix had been the lowest of her depression, a void she couldn't have seen the end of as alone as she had been. And he'd brought her back from the jaws of death. She didn't doubt he'd do it again if need be. Clearly, she was important to whatever his plans were, though she couldn't imagine them.

But even as she hated him for it, she was secretly glad for his presence. With him, even with everything that he brought, she didn't feel alone. It was odd how she had spent her life sharing her space with people and felt loneliest, but there she was alone and somehow not feeling as dejected. Knowing he was somewhere in the house made her feel . . . just feel. And it felt fucking good to *feel* again after going catatonic for so long.

She didn't realize when she drifted to sleep, but when her eyes opened next, a lamp was on by her side and it was dark outside. A cool breeze drifted in from the open deck doors, and Lyla sat up on the bed, rubbing the sleep from her eyes, watching the dark silhouette of the man leaning on the railing in the cold.

Keeping the softest, thinnest blanket wrapped around herself, she padded out to him, drawn like moth to flame, a moth that knew it would burn but unable to resist the pull deep inside.

It was very, very dark outside. The moon was a thin crescent in the sky, barely lighting anything. The mountains looked a little blacker than the sky and the waves barely glimmered, but their sound was loud, a soothing whoosh of water lapping against the shore. The wind was soft and cold on her face, and Lyla felt herself take in a deep breath, allowing herself to experience being outside like this for the first time. She still had an escort—she doubted he would let her be alone on the deck so close after she had tried to kill herself—but his presence wasn't that of a normal escort. She liked sharing this with him, and whatever his motives, he had given something precious to her.

"Thank you," she murmured quietly, her words low so as not to break the moment.

He didn't say anything, simply looked out into the dark, his elbows on the railing, hands hanging loosely from the wrist. She looked at what he was wearing—jeans and sweatshirt—and realized she'd never really seen him so dressed down.

He looked the most relaxed that she'd seen in her memory.

Questions bubbled inside her. "How long have you lived here?"

"A few months."

She took a step closer. "And how long have you had it?"

"About five years. It took a year to build."

That was a long time. Stepping closer to the railing, heart racing at the nothingness beyond, she gripped the blanket. "Why not live here before?"

He turned his neck to look at her. "You weren't here."

Her breath caught in her throat. She didn't know how to respond when he said things like that, like they were facts instead of lies that he fed her. Her heart, desperate for affection from him, wanted nothing more than to believe them, to believe the narrative he was spinning for her. But she had dealt with him for too long, she knew he was a master of manipulation and he knew which strings to pull for her, since she was an easy puppet.

Turning her face away, she didn't say anything. They simply stood in the dark for long, long minutes before he broke the silence.

"I don't understand emotions," he began, interlinking his fingers. "I never have. I don't find them particularly useful for myself, so I have never been attached to anyone either. People have been either useless or useful to me." He turned fully to sear her with a look again. "While you do fit my plans quite nicely, it's incidental. You'd be here even if you didn't."

Lyla felt her lips purse. "You're a liar."

"I am," he agreed without a pause. "But I don't lie to you."

A dark sound left her as hope, hope she'd thought dead and buried, resurfaced.

She saw his jaw clench at the sound.

A tense silence followed before he moved to the door. "I'll sleep in the other room until you invite me back. This bedroom is yours. This whole house is yours. There's food in the kitchen. Help yourself."

With that, he headed to the glass doors. "Oh, and don't try to kill yourself again. You're very close to getting a lot of answers you've been waiting so long for. You don't want to miss them, not this close."

Asshole.

Always dangling the carrot of truth in front of her. But he'd never explicitly told her that he would tell her soon, always pushing it to 'someday'. She didn't know if it was a line to hook her in or if he actually meant it. That was the thing with him—she never knew what he meant. But she was hooked, and the lure of answers was more than the lure of death, at least for the moment.

Shaking her head at herself, she followed him inside after a while, closing the glass doors behind her, realizing she was both dirty and hungry. First things first, she headed to the only black door in the room she hadn't opened, one tucked in a corner of the room on the other side of the closet. Assuming it was the bathroom, she went there.

The door opened into a short corridor—there were a few of those in this house, she realized—and opened into a bathroom unlike any she had ever seen. Her jaw dropped in shock, she stood rooted to the spot, frozen as automatic lights turned on behind a false ceiling with her presence, lighting the huge space in dim yellow.

It was black—like the other decor in the house—and metal and glass, the aesthetic screaming wealth and class. She had seen rich bathrooms, had spent her time soaking in many of them, but this was another beast entirely.

A panel of windows covered three quarters of the wall opposite to her, looking out over the sea, the other quarter covered by a large mirror. A black granite countertop held a black sink in front of the mirror—the kind without any cabinets behind it. The cabinets were under the counter, covered by dark wooden panels. In front of the windows, a shower space large enough to fit ten people was sectioned off with frosted glass. Another section with frosted glass held the toilet, a black toilet. She'd never seen that.

And in between the shower chamber and the sink, right against the windows, was a large sunken tub in the same black granite.

Blinking in awe for long minutes, it took her a while to actually move into the area.

Wow.

Wow.

Dropping the blanket near the entrance, she moved to the tub, looking over the fancy knobs. Looking at the tub brought back memories of other tubs, of water and the deadly lure beneath it.

She headed for the shower instead, stripping as she went. It took her a second to figure out the buttons on the panel but once she did, water began to fall down like rain, straight from the top.

Stepping under the hot spray, she felt the warmth seep into her muscles, relaxing her for the first time in such a long time a sigh escaped her. She stood under the spray long enough for steam to begin fogging up the glass. Content for the moment, she turned to the shelves in the corner for some shampoo and stopped. Tiny bottles—shampoo, conditioner, body wash—lined the shelf, different brands, different products, all sealed.

She stared at the shelf in wonder.

Not only did he know she liked the cute bottles, he was giving her options to try. Again. He was giving her the chance to experiment and see what she liked.

Who the hell was this man?

Shoving the question aside for later, she explored the different bottles, looking at each label, all the scents—jasmine, coconut, blossom, citrus, and the list went on. She picked the one that said 'peaches and cream' and poured a dollop on her hand, bringing it up to her nose.

Oh, she liked it. It smelled really nice.

Slathering it over her body, she scrubbed herself clean, taking the longest, most relaxing shower of her life. Using the same scent for the shampoo and conditioner, she spent a few glorious minutes enjoying the hot water, marveling that she could. In the complex, in all the houses she'd been in, showers had been communal, so finding any semblance of time and privacy had been out of question. This was such a novel experience for her that she took her time, staying under the cascade until her stomach growled.

Shutting off the water, she grabbed a towel from a stand outside and dried herself, wrapping it around and walking to the mirror. Fresh-faced and rested, she looked better than she had in months, though still too thin. The weight she'd lost over the months was visible in her protruding collarbones, and even on her face which had lost some of its roundness. Her shoulder length hair, though jagged, was much quicker to dry. Leaving it as it was, she left the bathroom, noticing the lights automatically turning off behind her.

She picked up the blanket from the floor and dropped it on the bed before turning right. Going to the closet, she explored, trying to find something comfortable she could wear, like a tank top or sleep shorts, but she couldn't find any. Hesitating, she bit her lip and looked around the wardrobe. There was no way she was going to sleep in any of the pricy clothes hanging there. No way. But what the hell was she going to wear otherwise?

Her eyes fell on a t-shirt he'd left folded at the bottom on his side, probably because it had wrinkles. Taking it out, she shook it open and quickly put it on. Foregoing any underwear—it wasn't like underwear was given a lot of priority in her experience—she found a hamper in the corner and left the towel in.

Barefoot, clean and dressed, she headed out of the room. The house was dark except for a few night lights. She quietly made her way to the kitchen, lights coming on as she passed by. It was so cool. but it took some getting used to. Automatic lights weren't a thing she had experienced. Good old switches to turn them on and off.

The kitchen, like everything in the house, was spacious and clean and modern, a lot of black and white decor interspersed with chrome. She went to the double-door refrigerator to see what it had, never really knowing how she'd cook anything because she hadn't ever cooked. The girls had been given sparse meals like rations throughout the day. She'd never even boiled water for tea. Did she even like tea? She'd never tasted it, so she didn't know.

But now that the thought was in her head, she went investigating. Going on her toes, she opened the cabinets one by one, her hunger sidelined for a moment. The first cabinet had neat jars with labels for each thing—flour, rice, pasta, and so on. It was the raw ingredient cabinet. The second one had all kinds of seasonings one could imagine. The third had plates and bowls and glasses on different shelves. But none had any tea.

Dejected, she rested back on her feet, her hands opening drawers and looking inside a little more frantically. So much stuff, but no tea.

It was the same with every single place she opened up. Stuff, stuff, more stuff.

But she needed the tea. She needed to know if she liked it, needed to prove to herself that she could boil water and brew it, that she wasn't completely useless.

Her lips quivered, and she gripped the counter, taking a deep breath to try to understand why she was feeling this, this odd tightness in her chest, this ball of emotion in her throat, so tight it felt like it would explode and destroy everything. Her arms began to shake with the strain of holding the counter, her breaths becoming choppy as her mind tried to make sense of this. Was this a lingering aftereffect of the drugs? Or was she breaking down? But why? Why over tea, of all things? Nothing had happened to her. She was in a beautiful place and there wasn't a sense of prevailing danger. Why then did her entire body feel like it would collapse in itself?

Her knees buckled, and she went down, her body shaking as the ball in her throat got heavier. Her nose started to burn, her eyes watering, her mind both mindless and mindful of every single second.

She didn't understand what was happening, and it was scaring her. This wasn't the black hole, this was something else, something unfamiliar.

She lay down on the floor, the cold marble comforting against her heated cheeks, shaking, sobbing, shivering, and she succumbed to blessed oblivion.

CHAPTER 13

LYLA

It was the sound that woke her up.

Sounds, to be precise. A loud noise, like the whirring of a machine and the chatter of two women.

She came to in the bed, her eyes blinking to adjust to the beautiful sunlight streaming in from the windows. The view, which had been majestic and dangerous yesterday, looked sublime and inviting today.

Jumping out of the bed, she walked to the deck, looking at the shimmering grayish-blue water of the bay and the magnificent rocky peaks, the sunlight on her skin warming her to the bones.

Taking in a full, deep breath, she turned on her heel and decided to begin her day by investigating what the noise was.

A deep red rose on the bedside table, one that hadn't been there the previous night, caught her eye. Picking it up, mindful of the thorns, she examined it, realizing it was a fresh cut and not an eternal rose. A note sat on the side.

'How do you like your home?'

Lyla blinked, reading the words again. Her home? No, he must've meant 'my' home and misspelled it.

Wondering what time it was and how long she'd been slumbering, how she hadn't heard him enter and leave the rose and the note, she walked out of the room, only to come to a halt at two females—a young girl and an older woman—in the area.

Immediately, her guards went up, making her realize how low she'd actually let them go within a day of being there. She wanted to demand who they were and what they were doing there, but her throat locked up. She couldn't talk to people anymore; strangers scared her. It was different when she was working—she knew what was expected of her then—but she didn't know what was expected of her now, and she didn't know how to react.

Without a word, she slowly started to retreat back into her room when the older woman glanced up at her, her face showing surprise.

"Good morning, Mrs. Blackthorne!"

She froze. *What the fuck?*

Startled at the address, she stared at the older lady in wonder. She didn't know if he had told them she was his wife or they had simply assumed, but for some reason, she did not correct her.

"P . . . please call me Lyla," she offered in return, stumbling but catching herself, the woman's warm smile making her feel strange.

"Yes, Lyla," the older woman accepted. "I'm Bessie, and this one here—" she pointed to the younger girl "—is Nikki."

Not really sure what the polite response was to small talk, since this was probably the first conversation she was having like this, she just gave them a small smile. It felt odd on her face, the sides lifting slightly, the muscles unused for so long. An awkward silence filled the space, before Bessie, blessed woman that she was, looked at her rose, her smile splitting her cheeks.

"I see Mr. Blackthorne has been using the garden. Have you seen it yet?" Lyla shook her head, and the older woman, maybe intuitive, maybe perceptive, didn't make any comment on her lack of reactions. She beckoned her forward with one hand, leaving aside the vacuum cleaner that she had been holding—the source of the noise. Hesitantly, Lyla walked forward, glancing at Nikki who stared at her with slightly cool eyes like the girls in the complex had.

"We hadn't even known he was married until a few days ago," Bessie kept talking, drawing her attention back. "He was always here alone, and we all just thought he was one of them bachelors, you know?"

"Who all?" Lyla asked, following Bessie as she led her to the main double doors of the house.

"The villagers mainly. When he bought this land and started building the house, gave lots of us jobs. I take care of the house. My husband takes care of the green, and Nikki takes care of the kitchen."

The calm, comforting way Bessie talked made Lyla relax a bit. "How many people . . .?"

"Work here?"

She nodded.

"About six," the older woman opened the door. "We're all day staff since the village is just a few minutes away. At night, there's only security at the main gate and those were brought from the outside by Mr. Blackthorne."

Fascinating.

The kind of man he'd always seemed, a lone wolf, she hadn't ever imagined him as having people working under him. But it fit him. He was commanding.

"Does he stay here all the time?"

The odd look Bessie gave her made her realize she'd slipped. If she were his wife, she'd know this already. Biting her tongue when the urge to overcorrect herself came, she turned to look outside and stopped short. A long porch wrapped around the house, stairs leading down to a pathway. One side of the pathway, the side that dipped down into the cliff, was completely paved with cement, a large honest-to-god black helicopter sitting there. A *helicopter.*

Mouth agape, she looked to the other side of the pathway, green lush grass beginning to span the slope, her eyes coming to rest on a glass shed a little way down.

"That's the greenhouse."

Of course, he had a *greenhouse.* She wouldn't be surprised if the next door she opened led to a throne room made of gold.

Surprised at her own sarcastic thought, she pulled up short, shaking her head. Sarcasm wasn't familiar to her, but it felt nice.

"Dr. Manson will be here tomorrow to see you."

Lyla blinked. "Who's Dr. Manson?"

Bessie gave her a warm smile as she led them to the greenhouse. "I'm sure Mr. Blackthorne must have told you."

He hadn't, but she bit her tongue not to give anything away.

And that was how her morning passed. Taking a tour of the greenhouse as Bessie introduced her to an older gentleman working there—her husband—and showed her where the property line was, quite far away from the house. The property was fenced with barbed wires, and she wondered for a moment if that's where he got the barbed wire from when he strangled Two and Three.

The dark thought was a good reminder that no matter how much finesse he showed to the world, how convinced Bessie and the staff were that he was a wonderful man—oh, he had them fooled—he was still the devil, and this was still her prison.

Bessie showed her where the tea was and showed her how to operate the tablet to look up anything she wanted. *'Mr. Blackthorne is so thoughtful.'*

That he was. He thought of everything and that's what made him so good. The staff was eating out of his hands, and Nikki wanted to fuck him. Had she fucked him? The thought unsettled her.

That was what she'd perceived in a day of being there.

Oh, and he had a helicopter on standby.

Still grappling with all the new information thrown her way, she shook herself.

Finally alone in the house after an insightful but exhausting day, she poured a cup of water in a pan and placed it on the fancy burner to boil. Bessie had showed her how to operate the dials, telling her that usually Nikki came during the day and prepared the meals.

The warring factions inside her were not quitting. One part of her wanted to escape and never see him again, the part that was angry and hurt and betrayed by him. The other part wanted to stay with him, be with him, actually find herself with him, the part of her that had fallen for the man over the years. But had she fallen for him or what he had represented—safety, power and control, all things she hadn't had?

She didn't know.

Looking at the tablet sitting on the kitchen counter, she opened it and typed into the search bar.

'Blackthorne'.

She got thousands of results, but nothing she could really find relevant to him. She tried again.

'Shadow Man.'

Same. Too inconclusive. She gave up.

Looking at the blinking cursor, she typed again.

'How to stop suicidal thoughts?'

Articles upon articles popped up on the screen, along with a helpline number that she couldn't call because she didn't have a phone. She clicked on the first article and read through slowly, her comprehensive speed not as fast as normal people.

#1. Talk to your friends or family.

She put the tablet down, breathing in through her mouth, her eyes welling up. She wouldn't be fucking suicidal if she had friends and family in the first place. All she had was him, and talking to him . . . she'd never really talked to him. Should she try? Forgetting the past, since this was her new reality, should she try for her own peace of mind?

Deciding she was going to do just that one day when she was ready, talk to the only person she could talk to freely, she turned to the now-boiling water. Blinking again, she turned the gas off and opened the search bar again.

'How to make tea?'

Following the steps, in a few minutes, she had the drink steaming in a mug. Adding a spoonful of sugar, terrified for some reason, Lyla brought the rim of the mug to her lips, taking a tiny sip.

And she fell in love.

She had made herself good tea.

One thing at a time.

Dr. Manson was an old, wrinkled dark-skinned man with sharp but warm eyes. He came calling the next day and sat in the greenhouse, and Lyla froze because she didn't know what to do.

"Bessie," the older man smiled at the woman accompanying her. "Would you please bring us some tea while I get to know the lovely Mrs. Blackthorne?"

"Lyla," she automatically corrected him, and the man gave her a gentle smile, asking her to sit on the chair in front of him. The greenhouse was sunlit and beautiful, and warm enough in the cold to sit comfortably in.

Lyla sat down gingerly, not knowing what to do or say as Bessie left.

"I'm a retired psychologist," Dr. Manson broke the silence after a few minutes. "My wife and I moved to Bayfjord many years ago, and while I don't see clients anymore, Mr. Blackthorne was very persuasive."

Lyla stared at him for a second, biting her lip. "What . . . what do you do exactly?"

"I help people deal with their mental issues."

She had mental issues. She knew that. "What kind of issues?"

Dr. Manson tilted his head to the side. "Whatever kind you want help with. But only if you want my help. Do you want my help, Lyla?"

Hesitantly, she nodded.

The older man smiled. "Great. Then know, that going forward, whatever you tell me will remain between us. Even though Mr. Blackthorne employs me, he won't know anything we discuss. Is that alright with you?"

It felt odd to be asked so many questions, like her choice in them mattered. She nodded again.

"Good. Then tell me anything about yourself."

Taking a deep breath, she began to stutter her way through some of her trauma.

It took her a few days to recover from the after-effects of the drugs. She slept a lot, day and night, and mostly stayed in her room, or sat on the deck watching the view unless Dr. Manson called her to the greenhouse every afternoon. While she hadn't talked to him about everything, even talking a little was slowly making her feel better. She told him about the tea incident, and he told her it was most probably an anxiety attack, that she would probably have more of them randomly until she gradually healed. He told her to talk to Mr. Blackthorne too, to try and find some middle ground between them, since she clearly cared for him.

Except Mr. Blackthorne was giving her apace. He came to her with trays of food, made sure she ate, and let her be. And for some reason, she both appreciated and abhorred that.

She took that time to come to terms with the fact that she had actually done something to end her life, and in the hole she had been, she didn't blame herself. But as the days passed, and she spent time alone in this beautiful place, somehow never feeling alone because she knew he was somewhere in the house, she also admitted that she didn't want to stay in that hole. She wanted to come out of it and she wanted to live. She wanted to experience beauty and feel like she belonged. She wanted to have him hold her and promise that she would never be hurt again. And knowing him, despite the last six months, she would believe him because she had the evidence of the last few years.

For the first time in a few days, she ventured outside the bedroom to find him on the couch watching TV. Hesitating on the landing, she tentatively walked over to where he sat with one muscular arm on the back of the couch, the other holding the remote.

At the sight of her, he muted the sound, but a couple kept kissing on the screen.

Fascinated, her eyes glued to the visual as she took a seat in the corner of the couch, she watched the man hold the woman's face in his hands, gently teasing her lips with his as airplanes flew in the background.

Throat dry, she asked. "What are you watching?"

"A romantic movie."

The answer, coming from him of all people, felt so ridiculous a bubble of laughter left her throat, the sound strangled halfway as she recognized it.

Her hand went to her neck, her eyes flying to him, only for her body to freeze as she saw the intensity of his gaze on her.

"I . . . laughed," she murmured, still stunned.

"Do it again."

"What?"

"I want to hear it again."

It was ridiculous. "I can't do it again."

Before she could blink, she was flat on her back on the couch and he was looming over her, one of his hands pinning her wrists above her head, the other on her ribs. Heart pounding, she gasped. "What are you doing?"

"Making you laugh again." With that, he began to prod the side of her ribs in quick motions that made her squeal and struggle to get away from him, sensations buzzing on her skin.

He was tickling her. The feared Shadow Man was tickling her.

The thought itself was so ridiculous, added to the motion of his fingers, that she began to laugh. "Stop, stop, stop, please!" She begged in between bouts of laughter, trying to move away from his hand but unable to in his hold, tears running down her cheeks with the intensity of her release, a high like never before buzzing in her head.

After long moments, he stopped, his hand stilling, both his hands coming to the side of her head, caging her in between as she caught her breath. His hypnotic eyes swirled with something hot, his face inches from hers as she stared up at him, her eyes flickering to his lips.

She remembered once thinking about her kiss, thinking about how intimate she wanted it to be. Her heart was still wounded.

The reminder sobered her.

"You hurt me," she whispered between them, her eyes welling up.

He leaned his weight on one arm, moving her short hair back from her wet cheeks with the other.

"I know."

An exhale left her at the acknowledgement from him, at knowing she was valid in feeling how she felt and he accepted that. He simply traced her tears with his thumb for a long moment while she took him in, his eyes on her eyes, his weight on her body, and felt something opening tentatively inside her.

"They broke me."

The words left her, and his thumb came to her quivering lower lip, steadying it, his intense eyes on hers.

"And they will pay."

The words, the exact words, he'd said to her before setting the man who'd drugged her on fire. The promise of vengeance and retribution she knew he would carry through, because he always had. Though he had left her for the last few months, he had been there through the years, and factions within her warred remembering both. It felt so long ago and it felt like yesterday.

Taking his dark promise to heart, she wrapped her arms around his solid weight on her, and pressed her face into his neck, breathing him in. It had been so long since she'd been held, so long since she'd held anyone, her body, her mind, her soul aching with the hunger of simply touching another and feeling safe. She was still not fully put together but slightly more than she had been in the morning. Maybe she would never be whole. But maybe, one day she wouldn't be as broken either. And that alone gave her some hope.

One thing at a time.

CHAPTER 14

LYLA

Dr. Manson was slowly becoming her favorite person. He had a weird sense of humor, one it took a while for her to understand, but he was kind and warm and genuine, and as she slowly talked to him, she felt herself opening more and more, even though she hadn't scratched the surface of her past with him. He knew she'd been raped and he knew she'd tried to kill herself, but beyond that, she didn't even know how to explain to an outsider. Yet, with what he knew, he was helping her.

It was dark outside, almost midnight, and she was watching TV in the quiet house—after searching *'best movies to watch for the first time'*—when the main door opened. Jolting up from her slumped, relaxed position on the couch, heart pounding, she pressed pause on the remote.

It had been a few days since she'd seen *him,* days since he'd told her there was something very important he had to do, and left her with the promise that he would return. She had expected to feel abandoned again, but for some reason, living in this house, getting into a routine, talking to Bessie and Dr. Manson, finding herself, she hadn't felt discarded. She had felt cared for, because the house, the staff, the doctor, he had made it all possible for her. Even in his absence, he had ensured that she would be looked after.

And she had missed him.

She had missed his heated, crazy eyes and his little notes and his roses and his quiet, solid presence. She knew from the time she'd spent observing him that he liked watching drama and romantic movies because the emotions fascinated him, and thrillers because he liked knowing answers before anyone onscreen did. She knew that he had meetings in the afternoons that he attended on his laptop while she met with Dr. Manson, and she knew he liked working out every morning at the crack of dawn. She knew he liked listening to her voice, and he liked that she was exploring more and more of herself.

He entered, wearing a hooded sweatshirt and jeans and boots, his mismatched, mesmerizing eyes finding hers. His gaze roved over her, checking her physically to see everything was right, finding her in his t-shirt. For a moment, she saw something like satisfaction cross his eyes before his face went neutral again. It had taken her a few days of living with him to realize that wasn't something he did on purpose to hide his expression—that was just natural for him. She had seen the way he put on masks when dealing with the staff, faking expressions she knew he didn't feel, and she realized she preferred him the way he was with her—real and without pretense.

Biting her lip, not knowing what to say even though she wanted to say so much, she asked the first thing that came to her mind. "Why do you have a helicopter?"

He turned to lock the door. "I like flying it."

"Is that how you got me here?"

His lips twitched with the memory of it. "Yes."

Lyla tried to remember anything about her transference, but it was all a giant blank.

"I need to take a shower so if you want to talk . . ." he left the words trailing and headed straight to where the bedrooms were. She scrambled and followed, turning the TV off behind her. The movie hadn't really been very engaging. Maybe she needed to find another list.

He went down the low stairs to the cave-like area and turned left to where the guest room was. Lyla bit her lip and followed, both curious and cautious. The small corridor opened into a smaller bedroom than hers, but still quite spacious, with a window looking at the sea and another door leading to the bathroom.

He dumped his bag on the bed, took off his leather gloves that hid his burned hands, and took his sweatshirt off, exposing a wide, unmarked back sculpted with muscles to her. Turning around, he let her look her fill of his chest and torso, his abs not bulging but sleek, a trail of hair arrowing down to his pants.

For the first time in months, arousal slivered through her veins, and she realized that while his physicality may have induced it, it was *him* she was aroused by. It was always him.

Her nipples tingled, wondering what his chest would feel like rubbing against hers, wondering if his arms would cage her in from the world or hold her down for his pleasure, wondering if he would stare into her soul as he claimed it or if he would suck it through her lips.

There was something wrong with her because after everything she had been through, the idea of being with a man, any man, being at his mercy and his control, should have made her sick. It did make her sick when she tried thinking about someone else. Not him. She wanted to be under him, struggling as he held her motionless, as he took what he wanted, ravaged her as he wanted. It should have made her sick but the thought of it lit a fire inside her.

Oblivious to the maelstrom within her, he sat down on the bed and unlaced his boots in quick movements, his fingers sure and strong and drawing her eyes, making her wonder how they would feel tugging her nipples, inside her, stretching her open, bruising her with his grip as he held her down, making her surrender to him.

What was wrong with her?

She'd had occasional fantasies of him, but nothing so intense, nothing so . . . *hungry.*

Finally done with the boots, he stood up and pushed his pants down, exposing his entire naked body to her for the first time, and she *froze.*

Not because he was naked, although he had an amazing body. Not because he was hard, even though the size of him was breathtaking. Not because he was letting her look, and his the confidence was a turn-on.

No, it was because along the ridge and the top of his massive cock, he was pierced. She had never, in her entire experience, even seen a pierced cock much less experienced one. And he wasn't just pierced, he was *pierced*—the underside, the crown, and the upper ridge.

What. The. Hell . . . ?

He moved to the bathroom without a word, and dazed, in shock, she followed him in. It was a smaller space than the master bathroom she'd used, without a tub and only a shower chamber.

Lyla looked at his ass cheeks, sculpted and hard, as he turned the spray on and got under it. Water sluiced down his back, his ass, his thighs and muscular calves before swirling into the drain. He took a dollop of shampoo and rinsed his dark hair thoroughly, in simple motions that somehow looked so good she wanted to feel him washing her. Gripping the counter behind her, she watched as he cleaned up, finally turning around so she could see his full frontal form.

His hard, huge, pierced cock bobbed with the movement, and saliva filled her mouth. A small part of her was sickened by her own lust, remembering how much she hated the appendage in her mouth. But she wanted his, she wanted to see how he would feel, how he would taste, how far he would go with that titanium jewelry.

His large, burned hand wrapped around his cock, suddenly making her realize how thick it was too. He would tear her apart and fuck if she didn't want him to. Years of attraction, of playing the push-and-pull, of fantasies she'd had with him, culminated in her mind.

Unbidden, mirroring his motion, one of her hands went to her aching breast, squeezing her nipple to find some semblance of relief.

"Hand down."

The command made in that deep, lower tone wracked her body with a shiver. Swallowing, she stayed where she was, not understanding what he meant.

"You want to see me do this?" he asked, tugging at his cock, and her eyes locked with his. She nodded.

"Then, no touching yourself. Get on the counter."

She complied, jumping backward. The granite felt cool against her heated body, the sink pressing into her back as she waited for him to tell her what to do.

His hand moved lazily on his cock, his hypnotic dual-colored eyes steady on hers.

"Spread your legs."

She was wearing his t-shirt—the one she had basically stolen from him—and silk shorts she'd put on after dinner. Heart racing, nipples so tight she could feel the heaviness in her breasts, she opened her legs, knowing she was wet and knowing he could see it on the damp spot spreading on the fabric.

His hand began to move faster over his cock, his other one pressed into the wall at his side, his eyes between her legs, to her nipples, to her lips, to her eyes again.

Her chest heaved as she watched him masturbate, his hand going up and down in a twisting motion. His chest moved more rapidly too, his light eye almost matching the other with his pupil blown wide, his hips jerking in the natural motion of sex.

"Say my name," he ordered her, and she suddenly blinked.

"I don't know your name." It was so ridiculous after everything they'd been through.

His hands paused on her words, their gazes locked as she held her breath.

"Dainn."

Dainn. Dainn Blackthorne.

She knew his name.

She remembered something he had told her once. "That's the name you got in the orphanage you were in?"

She could tell he was pleased that she remembered.

"Yes." His hand began to move again. "The old caretaker named me after death, so I gave it to him."

An exhale left her. *Dainn. Death.* Fitting too.

"Dainn."

A low sound, almost a growl, left him. The reaction sent a thrill down her body, merging with the heat, heightening it to another degree.

"Dainn," she said again, her voice breathy, remembering the effect he said her voice had on him. Boosted with a sudden sense of power, she spread her legs a bit wider. "Can you taste me on your tongue, Dainn?"

His breaths got choppier, his hand almost pulling his cock angrily now, veins in his neck beginning to bulge. Never, she had never seen a man more powerful and more wild at the same time, and the sight of him like this, knowing she was getting sides of him he didn't show everyone, made her headier.

A gush of wetness left her, all her senses aroused and teased to a pinnacle. She gripped the counter at her side to keep her hands in place, knowing he would stop if she touched herself. She couldn't bear it, not for too long. She hadn't felt pleasure in so long. "Dainn, please."

Within seconds, with another low sound, he came, strings of his cum washed in the shower and going down the drain. She watched it all, wanting to touch her own breasts, to push two fingers inside herself so badly she shook with it, the wet spot on her shorts getting wetter.

Moments later, once he caught his breath, his eyes flashed open and found hers. Like a jungle cat, sleek and deadly, he took a towel and wrapped it around his waist, coming toward her.

"Do you want me to touch you?"

She nodded vigorously.

The dark slash of a smirk came again. "I won't touch you, and you won't touch yourself either. Let it simmer."

What the fuck? She was going to explode.

"Trust me still?" he asked, his gaze piercing.

She recalled the question he had asked her before when she'd been drugged, a word that had tied them together since the day they'd met. She paused, thinking about it. Did she trust him still? Yes and no.

Her silence answered him enough.

His gaze intensified. "Good enough for now. You know where I've been the last few days?"

She shook her head, her arms trembling with the need wracking her body. His arms came to rest beside hers on the counter, caging her in without touching her.

"I found one of the three."

Her heart stopped.

She knew, immediately knew, what he was talking about. One of the three men who had abused her.

Her arousal began to simmer down at the memories.

One of his hands gripped her jaw, rooting her to the present. "I ended him." His nose found her nose, brushing it once in a gesture so soft she wanted him to do it again immediately. "I cut his hands off—" his nose went down her neck "—then his tongue—" down her breasts, his breath on her rigid nipples "—then his little dick."

All parts that had touched her.

She looked at the back of his head, his wet dark hair, and felt her throat tighten. Something blossomed inside her, unfurled, slowly, tentatively, terrified of being hurt again, being abandoned again, but still finding hope. Fucking hope.

"Was it the bald man or one of the other two?" she asked, her voice breaking, and saw him pull back.

His eyes locked with hers. "The one who had the camera."

Her body shivered with the mixed messages her brain was sending to it, oscillating between arousal and grief and rage and pain and arousal again as his words slowly penetrated her mind.

"You saw it," she whispered, horrified, humiliated.

He stepped between her legs, his hand tilting her jaw and his thumb tracing her mouth in a move she recognized instinctively as his.

"Every. Single. Second." His thumb pillowed her lower lip, his eyes intense on hers, his body pressed against hers, everything about him fierce and powerful and so dark she wanted it all for herself. "You didn't go through any of that alone."

Somehow, knowing he had seen it, that he had experienced it with her made her feel a little less lost. Knowing he had seen her be used and discarded, and knowing he still wanted her, it made something in her chest go tight in a way her heart bloomed. He had seen her at her worst, witnessed as they broke her, found her in the jaws of death, and somehow, he'd still found her worth saving. Even after all of it, he had brought her to his house and given her a safe space to heal.

Something in her fragmented heart softened.

They looked at each other for a long, quiet moment.

"I'm yours." It was sinking in, truly sinking in, how much his she was. A man didn't witness what he did everyday for her for no reason. He might not feel emotions as he said, but there was something solid, tangible, unbreakable between them, and they both knew it.

His nose brushed hers again. "All mine."

She could pinpoint the moment the course of her life changed six years ago. And sitting there on the countertop, six years later with the same man, with little slivers of secrets and silence, she knew the course of her life was changing again.

CHAPTER 15

LYLA

The next few days passed in adapting to her new life beyond her bedroom.

Waking up to the view of the beautiful mountains on one side and the sea on the other thrilled her every day. As did finding a fresh red rose and little notes on her bedside table. Notes that elicited different reactions in her.

The *'I got the piercings for you'* made her breathless.

The *'Did you know you snore?'* made her frown.

The *'I liked the dress you wore yesterday'* made her cheeks warm.

And so on and so forth.

Little notes, every single day.

She enjoyed the long showers she took, avoiding the bath mainly because of the memories she associated with being in a tub. She started using her tablet for everything. From searching *'how long should I boil pasta'* to *'is it normal for rape victims want to have sex again'* to *'best shows to binge'*? And the answers she didn't find, she asked Dr. Manson, who told her that yes, it was completely okay for survivors to want intimacy again.

Searches got varied, and life got a new routine. She tried different things and learned she had no talent for painting, didn't enjoy being online for more than a few minutes, and didn't like making jewelry. What she did like was cooking—or rather learning and experimenting—and reading, though she was a slow reader. And it wasn't a physical book from the library she was enjoying reading either, but one she'd found online and had Bessie help her buy. It had showed up on her search when she'd looked for *'raped heroine romance'*. She'd been skeptical that there wouldn't be many but surprisingly, and tragically, there were. It seemed being forced was more common than she'd thought, even in the outside world.

The book she was reading dealt with a normal woman who had been raped at a party, her struggles and how she fell in love again with a wonderful man. Parts of it, Lyla could relate to. Those parts—feeling dirty, hating her body, being depressed—those made her feel seen, acknowledged, like someone had reached inside her and told her it was okay to feel the way she did. But other parts—mainly where the heroine was falling in love with a gentle, caring man who told her how much he loved her and how beautiful she was every other page—she couldn't relate to.

She put the tablet down, staring out at the sea, imagining what it would be like. She imagined a good-looking, non-violent, gentle man, imagined him easing her into soft kisses, imagined herself sleeping with him for the rest of her life . . . and felt nothing. The more she was learning about herself, the more she was understanding that the love in the movies she watched with him wasn't something she'd ever understand.

The scene in her mind changed. She imagined herself running in the dark, getting caught by a man who was darkness himself, telling her she was his as he claimed her, making her feel safe and protected and unreachable for any other monsters. She didn't need a good man telling her he loved her; she needed a dark devil to tell her she was his.

And maybe Dainn was the man. Maybe he wasn't.

She shook her head. Who the hell was she kidding? She knew he was the man for her, had known for many years. Had she been trained by her brain to believe it? Probably. Was it 'healthy' like she'd read in articles? Probably not. But again, as Dr. Manson reminded her, other people's definition of healthy couldn't be hers. Her experiences were different, her past was different, and whatever made her grow and heal was healthy for her. All the information she'd been consuming over the days had been doing was simply making her think—think, so she could follow different directions of thought and decide for herself which she agreed with and which she didn't. She was discovering herself, slowly but surely, and that was all she could do. The knife on the counter still looked inviting sometimes, but she was working on it.

Getting up from the comfortable, plush armchair in the study, she went to the table and picked up the small notebook she had claimed for herself, opening it to the last entry.

'Cook pasta for dinner'.

One step at a time.

That's what she had begun to do at Dr. Manson's suggestion. Every morning, she wrote a task for herself to be done that day, and throughout the day, she focused on it. She'd read about it in one of the more useful articles on how to prevent suicidal thoughts as well, and it had been centering her more. Now, every time she had a thought, she opened the notebook and checked what she had to do that day, and eventually, the thought passed.

Checking the time, seeing the sun was setting already, she headed to the kitchen, the one place in the house she was slowly making her domain. Though she still wasn't an expert, she was experimenting more and more, looking up recipes online, seeing videos on how to cut a vegetable or slice the chicken, and she was becoming more and more confident about the simple, basic things. But only she had tasted her food, and it was the first time she was planning on making a full meal.

Dainn—she was still getting used to calling him that, both inside and out—wouldn't return home until late in the night. They had begun to share meals together, but if he was away, she usually ate and went to bed, mainly because she'd started waking up at the crack of dawn to simply enjoy the sunrise on the deck every morning. By the time she had dinner watching TV on those nights, she was droopy. Last night, she'd fallen asleep on the couch, only to come awake when he'd picked her up and carried her to bed, tucked her in, and left her sleeping.

She wanted him back in the master bedroom. She wanted to have sex with him, yes, but she also wanted more, much more. She wanted to fall asleep in his arms and wake up in them, she wanted to talk to him in the dark of the night and memorize his words for the day, she wanted to find his hypnotic, intense gaze on her in the morning and give him the reactions he wanted. She wanted it all with him. And maybe she was foolish—she more than likely was—but the desire to have him, to hold him, to hug him was a constant hunger under her skin.

She wanted to belong.

So, she got to work.

Putting her tablet on a stand in the corner of the kitchen, she put on a tutorial video even though she had practiced making it, and brought out the big pan. Putting the water on boil, she opened the fridge and brought out the eggs, tomatoes, cheese and butter.

Knowing what she knew about him being Shadow Man, she didn't expect him to come back early, but she was willing to sit up and wait for him. She did want to ask him what else he did and how he had all this wealth, ask him why he became the Shadow Man in the first place, ask him about what his big plan was that he'd once talked about. But he was closed off about those subjects, so she let him be for now.

Watching the video and following the steps, she lost herself in the motion of creating something. It soothed something inside her, just the simple act of cooking something from the scratch, and it excited something inside her, just knowing she was going to make someone beside herself eat it.

"Lyla."

The voice behind her made her turn. Nikki was putting on her coat, still aloof toward her. "Do you need anything before I leave?"

Lyla hadn't even known she'd been in the house. She shook her head, having brushed up on some basic manners. "No, thank you. Have a good night."

A smirk lit the other girl's lips. "Oh, I will."

Okay. That was odd.

"Oh, and whatever you do, please don't go into the greenhouse tonight." Nikki said on her way. "There's a storm coming."

There was something off about the way the girl said it. A weight that hadn't been there in days settled in her stomach. Her mood dampened, she quietly cooked her way through the meal, the scent making her mouth water. She put the servings on two plates and popped them in the oven to keep them hot, putting the rest in a serving bowl that she placed in the oven too. Then she cleaned all the pots and pans she'd used, setting them aside to dry.

And then, with everything done, she went to the closet, put on some warm leggings and a sweater, pushed her feet into sneakers, and walked out the main door.

The cold wind assailed her face as she looked at the dark sky. The moon and the stars were hidden behind thick clouds, and the helicopter was on the helipad, covered by something she couldn't see too well. The garden on the other side was dark too, everything except the greenhouse with one light on.

She couldn't see anything since the plants covered the glass. Tugging the sleeves of her sweater over her wrists, she briskly walked to the greenhouse, needing to know why the other woman had told her not to go there.

The ground was relatively flat on the cliff, just a gentle downward slope, and she covered it in minutes, slowly coming upon the main door that was open.

Her body froze.

Nikki stood naked in front of the long table, her hands holding Dainn's shirt, his hands on her waist.

Ice filled her veins as she took in the sight, her few weeks of relative happiness crashing as she realized she was discarded again. He hadn't touched her in all the days he'd had her under his roof, and that was because he'd already had someone. And Nikki had hated her on sight because she'd been with him.

God, she was an *idiot.*

Nikki's eyes came to her, triumph glistening in them, and Lyla exhaled through her mouth, unable to control the burn in her eyes.

Suddenly, his neck turned, his devilish eyes finding hers.

Lies. That's all they said to her. Lies.

She was *done.* He could eat the fucking pasta with Nikki and laugh over her feeble attempts.

Fuck him.

With that thought, she turned on her heel and ran down the hill, uncaring of where she was going, the only thought in her mind escape. Tears ran down her face, and she knew her reaction was not warranted. He'd never told her he was hers, only that she was his. He'd never told her that he'd not been with others, just like she'd been with others. The only difference, and the one that hurt the most, was that she'd never had a choice and he'd always had it. And for a moment, she had believed he had chosen her, but he'd not.

Plan. She was a part of his plan, and he was giving her only enough to keep her willing and under the illusion of happy.

Fool, fool, fool.

No, she would get to the village somehow, and hitch a ride somewhere, anywhere, away from all the emotional turmoil.

As her feet gained speed downhill, her lungs and legs burning due to the exertion she wasn't used to, something heavy tackled her from the back.

A scream left her throat as she went down, thinking it was a wild animal, and whatever the weight on her back was twisting at the last minute to save her the brunt of the fall.

Heart pounding in her ears, she caught her breath, struggling to get free from the weight that was under her, before suddenly finding her hands locked behind her back, her jaw locked in a tight grip, and her eyes locked with the devil's.

"What the fuck, Lyla?"

The tone of his voice made her still, the fact that he called her 'Lyla'—when it had always been *'flamma'*—making her realize he was *pissed.* And he was never pissed, not with her at least.

Thunder rumbled in the sky, throwing her back to the first time they had met in the dark, alone in the woods, with a storm coming in. That moment had changed her life, and she looked down at him, everything she'd been holding up for weeks, months, *years*, crashed inside her.

Every single time she'd been hurt, every time she'd been debased, every time she had hoped for something only for it to die, every time she had stared at the ceiling counting cracks, every time she had cried herself to sleep, every time she had given him a piece of herself only to feel discarded, every time she had lost parts of herself until she didn't even know who she was anymore.

Every. Single. Time.

Every. Single. Thing.

Every. Single. Memory.

Crashed, collapsed, crushed inside her.

She *shattered.*

She felt her shoulders shake, her chin quivering, the old tears on her cheek joined by others, and she tilted her head back, screaming her pain to the sky.

And it felt *glorious.*

She screamed and screamed and screamed until her throat felt raw, crying and thrashing, for minutes and hours she didn't know. She cried and cried until she couldn't anymore, until her breath got short and she began to hiccup.

The black hole opened wider inside her mind, asking her to fall into it again. It didn't hurt when she went into the black hole, she didn't feel the pain tearing at her when she was consumed. She slowly felt herself succumb, wanting the numbness it brought her, if only for a while.

"Shh. It's okay, *flamma.* It's okay. Shh. You're safe."

Words penetrated into her consciousness, a litany of words spoken right into her ears, pulling her away from the black hole.

She resisted, keeping her eyes closed, wanting the numbness.

"My beautiful girl," the voice kept whispering, seductive in its call, alluring in its lure to reel her back in. "So soft, so vulnerable, so hurt. You hurt, don't you?"

She did. She hurt, and she didn't know how to heal. She'd thought it had gotten better, but it had been an illusion. Would she ever get better? Would it ever not hurt?

"I will set the whole world on fire before I let anything hurt you again."

The dark promise full of violence made the black hole take a step back.

"Give me your eyes, *flamma.* I want to see the fire in them. Show them to me."

The two forces warred within her, the black hole pulling her to oblivion and the devil holding her tight, refusing to let go.

And suddenly, her hands were free.

That sent her eyes flying open, the sudden loss of the touch that had been anchoring her imbalancing her.

She blinked as he stood. Bending to pick her up in his arms and nestling her close, he began carrying her back to the direction of the house.

Jolted from whatever mental state she had gone in, she hiccupped occasionally, slowly letting her mind come back down to reality, unable to understand her heightened emotions or her overreaction. And she had overreacted, hadn't she? She had found him fully clothed with a naked woman and done the first thing that had come to her mind—run. She hadn't given him the benefit of the doubt, hadn't waited to calmly let him explain exactly what had been going on, hadn't even stayed to let him get a word in.

And then she'd screamed like a banshee and proceeded to have a mental breakdown in the middle of nowhere.

She'd been doing so well, so much better. She just didn't understand it.

Embarrassed that he'd witnessed something like this again, witnessed how broken and imperfect she was, she hid her face in his neck, her body trembling in the aftermath.

Their walk back passed in utter silence, and she took the time to steady her heart-rate.

They emerged near the greenhouse just as cold, fat drops of rain began to pour.

"Hold on tight," he instructed her before suddenly turning her so she was over his shoulder. World tilted upside down, she held onto his jacket as he sprinted back to the house, the torrential downpour soaking them both within seconds.

He didn't stop under the porch, simply opening the door and carrying her inside, all the way to the master bathroom.

Slowly setting her down on the floor, he pushed her wet hair out of her face, looking down at her with a softness she'd never seen from him.

"Get out of the clothes."

The instruction came on the heel of him pulling away, leaving her standing alone in the bathroom.

Confused, she did as he'd asked, dropping the wet clothes to a corner of the floor, before taking a shaky breath and splashing water on her face.

They both sucked at emotions it seemed, her with the excess of it and him with the lack. And she had to bridge the gap, or at least try to, so something like tonight didn't happen again. Though, it probably would. Dr. Manson had warned her it could, but she had fallen into a sense of security, and it had caught her unaware. But she could hope it wasn't as often, because she felt raw, her wounds that had been closing torn open again. And every time this happened, she would have to start from the scratch to try to stitch them together, each time making the scar deeper and worse.

Walking out into the bedroom naked, she found herself pulling on the silky bottle-green shorts and camisole set she'd put on the bed for the night before going out. Running her fingers through her hair, noticing the way they were beginning to fall more into their natural waves, she exited into the open living area.

The smell of the pasta she had made, what felt like ages ago, wafted from the kitchen.

Following her nose, she went into the space she had slowly made her own, and found him sitting on the dining table, shirtless in his sweatpants as he liked to be when he lounged around at home, his hair wet and gleaming in the low lights.

The plates she'd put in the oven were on the table, along with two tall glasses of water.

"Sit."

Suddenly nervous, both because that was a meal she'd made and because of the breakdown she'd had, she quietly took a seat on his right, tucking her chin into her neck.

"What happened tonight?"

His quiet words, spoken low but clear, made her steal a glance at him. She wet her lips, finding the courage to open the door for some honest, real communication. That meant being vulnerable again, but at this point, she didn't think she had much to lose.

"Seeing her there … with you … it triggered something," she admitted haltingly.

He took a sip of his water, his plate untouched. She knew he didn't much like alcohol. She didn't either, and the glass of water in front of her told her he'd noticed as much.

"What did you feel?" he asked, his hypnotic dual eyes snaring her in its trap. *What did she feel?* He didn't experience emotions as she did, and knowing he wanted her account of her feeling things made her heart race.

"I felt—" she stopped, looking at him, her throat working "—angry. So, so angry."

"Why?" he prodded, leaning slightly toward her.

"Because I thought you'd chosen her," her voice wavered with her words. "I thought you were keeping me on the side, making a fool out of me, giving me little nothings and giving her everything. I felt angry. I felt hurt. I felt *jealous.*"

"Why?" he pressed, not letting go.

"Because you're mine!" She slammed her hands on the table, standing up. "You're the only person, the only thing in this entire world that is mine!" Her chest heaving, she glared at him. "*My* killer, *my* stalker, *my* lover. The thought of sharing your obsession makes me sick to my stomach. You have power over me. Is that what you wanted to hear? That your claim makes me an idiot because my stupid fucking heart believes you? Is that it?"

She looked down at him as he sat back, a satisfied expression on his face.

"Flamma."

One word. Just one word and everything felt right in the world for a second. She took a deep breath, calming herself. Taking her seat again, she gulped down the water in her glass, aware of him watching her.

"Your heart isn't stupid." His words, again quiet, made her look at him. "Soft, yes. Stupid, no. I think it's quite smart to believe me when your mind doesn't."

She didn't know what to say to that.

"There's been no one for six years, Lyla."

His words made her straighten in her chair, the disbelief evident on her face.

His lips twitched. "Believe me or don't, fact is fact. I haven't fucked anyone in six years. I've not touched anyone who's not you in six years. And I've never kissed a woman on the mouth in my life. Never saw any point in it."

Lyla stared at him, dumbfounded. "I don't understand."

He simply shrugged. "Any other woman would have been a poor replacement for you, and it didn't seem worth the effort. Now, tell me, am I lying to you?"

Lyla observed him, his neutral face as he let her weigh her opinion. Her mind told her he could be manipulating her, telling her things she wanted to hear so she'd fall for his traps more easily. But her heart, the stupid beating organ in her chest, it said something else.

"No," she whispered, shaken by the fact that he'd been with no one.

"Good girl."

"I've not kissed anyone too, not by choice."

Her confession fell between them and she saw him look at her mouth. "Then, when you choose, it'll be mine."

A sigh left her.

She looked down at her plate of pasta, and slowly took her first bite. It tasted pretty good to her, but she didn't know if her taste buds were reliable at all. Watching him take his bite, her grip on her fork tightened.

His face showed no reaction, but he chewed slowly, looking down at the plate before bringing his eyes to her. "Did you make this?"

Nerves fluttered in her belly. "Yes. I watched a video and practiced a few times with smaller portions before making this. I . . ." she hesitated. "I wanted to make a nice meal for us." Her eyes lowered.

His hand came to her jaw, bringing her face back up. "Make us a meal whenever you want. You're gifted at this."

"You like it?" She didn't know why she needed his approval, why it mattered, it just did.

"Yes."

A sigh of relief left her as her confidence bloomed. '*You're gifted at it.*' She was good at something.

They finished the meal in companionable silence.

Since the moment felt true, honest, open, she risked asking him the one thing that had always blown up in her face. "Is he . . . is he okay?"

She watched him as he finished his last bite and stood up, taking both their plates to the sink, soaking them in. She took a towel and stood beside him, waiting for him to answer.

"Yes, he's okay."

Something heavy she hadn't known had been inside her lightened a bit.

"You've been keeping an eye on him, haven't you?" she asked, needing to know he was watching over, looking after the one thing between them.

"I have. Just like I've been keeping an eye on you."

Relief unfurled in her belly. When the Shadow Man decided to watch over someone, they were safe.

Overcome with emotion, she impulsively stepped into his back and wrapped her arms around his middle, feeling him still with the plates in his hand.

"Thank you," she whispered into his back, her voice quivering with so much feeling she felt her chest overflowing with it. "Thank you so much."

He turned around within her embrace, taking a hold of her face in his hands, his dual eyes blazing on hers. "For you, *anything*."

He brushed their noses together in the lightest of kisses, the sensation burning through her entire body. Lyla could not remember being embraced by anyone, had no memory of feeling as safe as she did right then.

"Hold me, please."

His hands tightened around her and he pulled her in, her face going into his chest, her nose filled with his distinctive, masculine scent, her body full of the warmth of his. He held her close, and listening to his heartbeats, feeling everything she was feeling, she could almost believe he felt it too.

CHAPTER 16

HIM

He had to tell her about her brother, about who she was. But she wasn't ready yet. With the way her mind was grappling with her life and reality, something like this could break her. He had asked Dr. Manson about it, asked her if revealing her past would help her progress, and he advised against it too for the moment. She was fragile at the moment, still hurting, still healing, and he needed her fully ready to handle it when she learned the truth.

And he was selfish. He knew if she knew she had a family, a brother who had been looking for her for over twenty years, she would eventually go to him. And he couldn't have that, not until he was certain that she would return of her own will back to him, because the only other option would mean abducting her from Caine and making them all his enemies. And while he didn't give a fuck about their enmity, the rift would end up hurting her in the friction, so he would rather avoid it. He didn't like her hurt.

He watched from the shadows as Tristan and Morana talked to the child psychologist he had sent their way unbeknownst to them, an old student of Dr. Manson. Morana was listening more animatedly than her lover. He liked Morana as much as he could like another human being. She was smart, determined and stubborn, and she knew how to look out for herself. He respected all of those in a human being. That's what made them interesting to maneuver. She also seemed to be genuine, something he was glad for because Tristan was the biggest threat to him. Not because he was more powerful or more lethal, but simply because he had a connection and devotion to Lyla that she craved. A better man would let her go and let her find some happiness with another. A better man would let her go and let her satisfy her cravings somewhere else.

He wasn't a better man. Fuck, he wasn't even a good man.

And once upon a time, he might have let go of her. But not now. Not when she'd run from him and roused the animal inside him he hadn't known he'd had. Not when she'd shattered in his arms and let him anchor her and bring her back. Not when she'd given him another piece of herself, trusting him to keep her safe. She had cooked him a meal like he was special, embraced him like he was someone worth holding, and looked at him with emotions a demon of death like him had never seen, and certainly didn't deserve.

It was the little things—the way she broke down over tea in his kitchen and put herself together again, the way she thirsted to learn and constantly be better for herself, the way she forgave him and let him in. It was the way she staked a claim on him and the way she trembled for his touch, the way she didn't run when he told her of the death he wreaked for her, the way she accepted his soulless form into her soft heart. It was the way she stole glances at him, the way she stole his t-shirts, the way she stole parts of him too.

There was no fucking way he was ever going to let go of her.

He had long left obsession and entered into a whole new territory, one he didn't even recognize because it was *more.*

More obsessive. More intensive. More possessive. *More.*

If he'd been ready to burn the world for her before, it was nothing compared to the destruction he would cause now.

And though he had no plans to keep her from Tristan, he needed to be sure that she wouldn't leave him in the dust when the time came.

The world wasn't ready for what he would unleash if that ever happened.

CHAPTER 17

LYLA, 6 YEARS AGO

Thunder rumbled in the sky and she ran as fast as she could, the little bundle wrapped in a blanket in her arms, her face streaming with tears as her lungs burned. She was sore and hurt between her legs, and she was pretty certain she was bleeding, but she wouldn't have gotten another chance.

The bundle in her arms cried at being jostled.

She cried with him.

For the nine months that she had carried him in her young womb, the beautiful product of a ghastly, horrific act, she had vowed to herself that she would get him out. She knew what they did to the children born in this hell, how they took them and began grooming them before they could even speak properly. And she had vowed, no matter what happened, her child would not grow up in the hell she had. Somehow, someway, she would get him out or die trying.

And with the pain between her legs increasing, the weakness

in her body from the aftermath of the delivery making her mind dizzy, she knew that was very likely. But if she had to die, she would die after getting him to some semblance of safety. She just had to stay away from the main roads they used, and hopefully end up on another. There had to be someone in the world who could help her.

Pausing to catch her breath, she leaned against a tree, swaying her little boy in her arms to calm him down a bit. She didn't know a thing about being a mother, wasn't sure if she'd ever make a good one, but there was one thing she could give her baby and she would die trying for it.

She held him for a moment, heaving in large breaths, and scanned the area for her next path.

Knowing she couldn't rest for more than a few minutes, the risk of security already scouring the woods too high, she began to run again and run hard, the thin soles of her shoes barely any protection. She would have blisters on her feet but it would be worth it if he could be safe.

Get him out. Get him out. Get him out.

With the words repeating in her mind as a mantra, she kept jogging, feeling the wetness between her legs, noticing the woods thinning out eventually. It could mean there was civilization close by, which could mean there was help. A burst of energy filling her at the thought, she headed to the place where she could see the woods opening onto a street of some kind.

Stopping again to catch her breath, she looked around feverishly.

There was a street and one building, nothing more, and one car loitering. She recognized it as one of the complex security's. They were patrolling, probably searching for her.

Pulling back into the shadows of the trees, turning to run again, she bumped into something hard.

Already dizzy from the weakness and dehydration and blood loss, she began to fall, her arms instinctively tightening around her bundled boy, just as two large hands clamped on her waist, steadying her.

"Easy, girl."

At the sound of the voice, she tilted her neck up to see a tall man, probably in his late twenties, with mismatched eyes looking down at her. She'd never seen eyes like that on anyone.

"Help me," she croaked through her dry throat, her weight leaning on him. "Help me, please."

A visible shiver wracked his frame before he looked at her, properly *looked* at her.

"What do you need?" he asked, the seriousness of his tone making her feel a little more sure about her decision. She studied him as best as she could, an instinct within her telling her to trust him.

Lifting the bundle in her arms, she spoke. "Take him. Take him away from here, somewhere safe where he will grow up with love and care. Please. They're coming for me, and he needs to be away when they find me. Please, please, please . . ."

The man's mismatched eyes drifted to the baby swaddled in the thin blanket. "Is he yours?"

She nodded, her eyes tearing up again, the pain of giving him up a burden she would carry gladly for his chance at a better life.

The man stared at her then, deeper, so deep she felt he was searching her soul.

"You would trust me with your child?"

The question made her pause, but the instinct inside her, the one that had run with her baby in the first place, remained steady, unwavering.

Hugging her child one last time, she pressed a kiss to his forehead, her chin quivering, and handed him over to the man.

"I will trust you with him. But promise me—" she cried out as the pain in her insides increased, cutting off her words. She took a deep breath and continued. "Promise me you'll keep him safe. If you can't keep him, send him to someone who will love him. Promise me."

Thunder rent the sky, rumbling loudly in the clouds, echoing her pain.

He held her son in the crook of his arms, his head tilted to the side as he stared at her with something close to fascination.

"I promise. He will be safe."

Her knees buckled in relief and he wrapped an arm around her waist, holding her steady with one hand while holding her baby with another. The support of his strong arm broke her then. She began to sob hysterically into the chest of this strange man, holding onto the lapels of his jacket, crying for everything she was losing and the unexpected support she had found.

"What's your name, *flamma?*" he asked her softly, and she looked up at him, surprised at the word he'd used, not knowing what he meant.

"Lyla."

"Endless night."

Is that what it meant? Endless night? Fuck if it didn't fit her life.

A shout from the woods made her straighten urgently.

"Please leave," she urged the stranger. "Take him. Now!"

Her eyes flitted to the round face peeking from the blankets, agony searing her as she leaned down to kiss his cheeks again, not knowing if she would ever see him again, not knowing what his fate would be but trusting the only choice she had.

"Be safe, little Xander," she murmured against his soft cheeks. "Be strong. Be loved, my beautiful baby."

The man stayed still for a long second, watching her as she said her goodbye, before turning on his heel and walking into the darkness with the only thing she loved in the world.

PART 3

FLAMES

"How can you become new if you haven't first become ashes?"

—Friedrich Nietzsche

CHAPTER 18

LYLA | PRESENT DAY

She jerked awake at the dream, her heart racing as thunder rumbled in the sky outside. She hated thunderstorms. As a child, they had scared her, and as an adult, they reminded her of the night she had lost her most precious gift—her son.

She had been close to eighteen when one of the men in the club had impregnated her, and though the child had been the result of a rape, it had been *hers.* She had spent months connecting to him, loving him, talking to him, and accepting that he would never know her. The night she had gone into labor, there had been a storm, and after hours of unimaginable pain, he had come screaming into the world.

The doctor had cleaned him up and swaddled him for her to feed, but she hadn't. She had only seen the storm, known that most of the people on the grounds would be under shelter, and she had run.

Run straight into the arms of the man who would change both their lives.

After that night, she had never expected to see him again. But less than a week later, he had showed up at her work.

And again.

And again.

Until he became a fixture in her life, an anchor in the hurricane, a rock against the waves. Until he started leaving a trail of bodies of everyone who tried to hurt her. Until he claimed all the broken pieces of hers as his own.

She wondered why she had dreamed of their first meeting tonight. It could have been the storm, or the fact that he'd talked about Xander for the fist time, or the fact that he'd held her like he had that night. Whatever it was, need, pure, unadulterated need, overpowered her.

Unable to stand it any longer, she moved on silent feel to the door, going out and to the guest room, her heart pounding, but telling her it was *right,* the same instinct that had made her trust him all those years ago telling her to do it again.

Close to his door, she inhaled deeply and opened it, just needing to take a peek if he was asleep.

He was.

Arm thrown behind his head, another on his stomach, eyes closed and face restful.

Hesitating on the threshold, she simply watched him, the need inside her a turmoil.

Quietly, without making a sound, she tiptoed into the room, going around his bed, her eyes on his face in the light from the outside.

This man, as dark and dangerous and defective as he was, was hers.

She leaned down slowly, pressing her lips to his for a second, feeling his breaths on her face as his soft mouth against hers, before she pulled back.

She turned to leave, right as a hand ensnared her wrist in a steely grip, making her heart pound as she looked to find him wide awake, his eyes alert, intense, heavy on hers.

He waited patiently for her to break the silence, and finding the courage from somewhere deep within her, she did.

"Make me yours."

He was up from the bed, tipping her into his arms in one fluid move like he'd been waiting for her, taking her to the master bedroom as she gripped his shoulders.

The room remained dark, only the little moonlight coming in through the glass doors lighting up the space.

Drunk on the dream, the emotions from the last few days, hell the last few years, she tilted her head to look at him in the moonlight—her dark devil who owned her soul.

"I was reading a book yesterday," she whispered in the space between them, not knowing any finesse to say it any better. "The man in the story found the woman and said he would make love to her." She swallowed. "Will you make love to me tonight?"

She knew he could see the earnestness in her eyes, the hunger for this affection in her face, the desire for this intimacy in her voice. He set her on her feet.

"What did the man do to make love to her?" he murmured, taking a step forward as she took one back.

She looked into his eyes, those mismatched eyes that had held her captive since the first time she saw them, and gave voice to the deepest desire of her heart.

"He touched her soul."

He took a hold of her jaw, pulling her up until she stood on her toes, his lips a hair-breadth from her. She didn't know if he didn't close the distance between them because he'd never kissed or because he never wanted to, but she waited. They just breathed each other in for a long moment, before he leaned forward and brushed their lips together in the lightest of kisses, so light the sensation made her strain higher to get more.

"If we do this," he said quietly against her mouth, "I will be your last everything. You choose this, you choose everything I am, every twisted, deranged, obsessed part of me. You choose this, and I will never fucking let you go. Do you understand?"

Her eyes fluttered close. "I do."

Before the last word was out from her lips, his mouth slashed down over hers.

Mint. Coffee. *Him.*

She strained her toes to take her as high as she could go, her hands clinging to the width of his shoulders, one of his hands on her jaw, another on her hip, holding her upright. He pulled back, his eyes dark, the pupil of the light one blown as he gave her a heated look, before he dove in again, picking her up with one hand and turning so her back rested against the closet door. She wrapped her legs around him, grinding against the rock-hard bulge in his sweatpants as he devoured her. The taste of him exploded on her mouth, and she opened hers.

Tentatively, she swirled her tongue against his.

And the most unexpected thing happened.

He *shuddered.*

A full body, uncontrolled shudder.

She pulled back to find his eyes on her, a slightly unhinged look in them that she'd never seen before as he demanded, "Do that again."

Feeling her heart pulsing through her entire body, her nipples stiffened to tight points against his chest, just separated by a thin fabric, she pressed herself closer to him, gliding her hand into his hair and tugged him into her.

She ran her tongue over his lips and he pulled her into his mouth, sucking on it in a way that had her pussy throbbing against his cock, her body beginning to writhe with sensations, a blaze of fire spreading inside her.

They stood there for a long time, kissing, testing, tasting, learning each other's mouths. He shuddered again when their tongues glided over each other, and she felt the jolt of it straight between her legs, knowing it was she who was responsible for such visceral responses from him. Their first and second and third kisses merged into one as he held her up, taking, owning, claiming every inch of her mouth.

Still kissing her, he moved, and suddenly, she found herself lying on her back on the bed.

He pulled away from her mouth. "Trust me still?" he asked, and she gulped, before she gave a nod.

His lips twitched. "Do as I say and you'll get a gift."

God, she loved it when he said that.

Putting one hand on the bed by her side and another under her waist, he single-handedly pulled her up the bed, until her head rested on the pillow. He hopped down from the bed with agility, pushing his pants down, his cock springing out, the piercings glinting in the moonlight.

"Hands above your head," he instructed her, and she complied, curious to see what he had in mind. "Don't move."

With those words, he walked out of the room.

Lyla stared at the ceiling, then turned to look at the darkness outside, waiting for him to return. Minutes passed. She became aware of the way her breasts thrust up in this position, her nipples pointed out prominently, her stomach exposed, her pussy weeping in her shorts.

"Dainn," she called out after what felt like eternity, and he didn't come.

Whimpering in need, she writhed on the bed but didn't pull her hands down, wanting whatever gift he had in mind.

After a long time, he entered again, his eyes warming at finding her in the same position. "Good girl."

Something within her preened under the praise.

"When we are together, you trust me. In here, you let go completely," he told her, tracing her mouth with his thumb. "This will get intense for you, and you will tell me to stop. But I won't stop. I'll push you. Are you okay with that?"

Her pussy clenched at the thought, the thought of her begging him to stop and him going on anyway. "Why do I want this?" she asked, trying to understand. "I shouldn't."

"Because you know you're safe here."

The words, his words, stated in the most factual of tones while he watched her made her pause. He was right. She wanted to beg, to be taken completely, because she knew she was safe. She knew that he wouldn't hurt her. It was the fantasy of it, the idea, the liberation.

At her acceptance, taking a hold of her camisole, he ripped it down the middle, the sound loud in the room, escalating her heartbeats. He pulled the scrap of fabric up her raised hands and tied a knot, leaving one long end hanging.

Her heart began to pound, bondage never something that had brought her anything but anxiety. "I don't have good experience being tied up."

"I know."

Looking at him, she bit her lower lip, slightly apprehensive, mostly aroused. He pulled her shorts down, throwing them away, leaving her naked on the bed.

"Spread your legs."

She did without hesitation, loving the way he looked at her with intense possession and incredible heat. He traced her opening with his middle finger. "So wet. So needy. Do you want my cock, *little flamma?*"

"Yes."

"Yes, what?"

"Yes, Dainn."

His finger entered her, and she clenched around him. It had been too long since she'd cum, and her body was primed, ready for it. He moved his fingers inside her expertly, scissoring to stretch her out for his cock, his thumb strumming her clit, sending wetness gushing out from her.

She cried out as he added a third finger, her hands unable to move.

"You remember the first time I touched this pussy?" he asked, cupping her firmly.

"Y . . .yes," she exhaled in a shaky breath. It had been after he had sliced people open in the maze. He had found her, looked upon her body, and cupped her just like that with his gloved hand.

"What did you feel then?" The words kissed by seduction fell upon her ears.

"Scared, confused . . . excited," she recalled.

"Are you scared, confused now?"

"A little."

"Good."

Within moments, with his eyes on her body and his fingers inside her, she could feel the heat cresting, rising and rising and rising, hurtling her toward a glorious climax.

But his hand stopped.

She cried out as he removed his hand, both in anger and surprise, and realized he had climbed on the bed to get between her legs instead. She split them open as far as she could, eager and willing and more ready for a man than she had ever been.

His cock looked scary in the moonlight, and the idea of having it, of finally having him, thrilled her.

The tip of his cock kissed her pussy lips, the coolness of the piercing a huge contrast to the heat of him, and she writhed her hips, her walls clenching emptily, needing him to fill her. Her hands locked above her head, her hips held down by his palm, the lack of movement only sent more heat spiraling inside her. He stayed still, and she rotated her hips, trying to get him to slip inside, one of his hands pushed her immobile, his eyes taking all of her in.

The wait was killing her.

"Fuck me," she begged, not caring that the desperation in her voice far exceeded any before.

His lips twitched. "I thought you wanted me to touch your soul?"

The amusement in his tone pushed her frustration higher. "Fucking rip it at this point. Just move, please."

He didn't, teasing her, toying with her, and a sob escaped her chest, tears of sheer need, sheer frustration, of having satisfaction so close but unable to get it.

"Another man wouldn't have made me wait so long," she taunted him, knowing she was playing with fire but knowing no other way to trigger him. He was possessive of her, and that was the only point she could think of.

He let her hip go and took a hold of his cock, slapping it against her clit in punishment for her words, and the sensation made her slicker than she was. She was primed, absolutely primed, so swollen with need she could feel herself throbbing.

"Another man wouldn't have had you so wet with need you drench the bed." His low words filled the space between them. "You're needy for *me.*"

"*I am,*" she admitted. "I need you, Dainn. I need you so much. All of you. Please. Take me. Claim me. Own me."

With a slight rumbling sound, he pressed his thumb to her clit.

And then he pushed in.

Right as she began to come.

Her eyes rolled to the back of her head, a sensation like nothing, *nothing*, before shaking her entire body, the pressure of his entry and the rippling of her walls and his thumb on her clit shooting her arousal higher, drawing out her orgasm to a point it felt endless.

He was thick and long and heavy, slowly easing inside her, the jewelry on his cock sliding in over tissues she didn't even know she had, eliciting sensations from every single inch of her swollen pussy until it felt on fire. She was gasping, stunned at the feeling of this, at the feeling of him, unable to believe that he'd done this just so he could give her this experience and make himself feel like her first.

With the way she was stretched and the way she was stimulated, *nothing* could have compared to it.

She looked at his eyes, seeing his gaze on the place he entered her body, his piercing-covered cock slowly disappearing into her little pussy until he was all the way in, throbbing inside her, and god, she throbbed with him. Hands tied above her head, impaled by him, she felt owned, taken, possessed, and she loved every second of it, loving the surrender of herself to the claim of him, loving the way he fit her.

He held still as she came down from her orgasm, letting her walls adjust to him.

And then he *moved*.

A noise more animal than human escaped her chest, her eyes clenching shut at the intense sensation straddling between pleasure and pain. He echoed the noise with his own low growl, one hand on the headboard holding one end of the torn camisole that tied her hands, the other on her clit, rubbing and rubbing and intensifying the sensation to too much.

It was *too much*.

She couldn't take it.

"No," she mewled, trying to move her hands, but it was locked in place. He didn't stop, pulling out so slowly she felt every tissue moved by him and his titanium, a spot inside her being pushed by one of piercings in a way that made stars explode behind her eyes. A fire started from the point, spreading out through her blood, her muscles, her entire body lit up like a supernova until it built and built and built and *exploded.*

She heard herself screaming until she couldn't, the sensation so intense her muscles began to spasm, her heart thundering, her spine arching up until she thought her back would break.

She came down, barely, before he thrust inside her again, hard, continuously rubbing her clit, and she began to beg.

"Too much, it's too much, please, oh god, Dainn please . . . stop, no, no, too much . . ." it became gibberish as the supernova exploded again, leaving her a shaking mess while he continued to thrust in and out of her, hard, steady, *deep,* so deep it was almost painful but oh so good.

"One more, *flamma,*" she heard him say. "Give me one more."

She shook her head vigorously, knowing she would die if she came again. It was too intense, too much.

No. Yes. No.

But she had surrendered, and he commanded her body, finding dark places within her she'd never explored before, owning them, taking them, telling her it was okay for her to have them.

Her eyes clenched shut as he took over her body, and she shook, never having felt so much sensation through a body she had hated.

A whirring noise from somewhere above broke through her daze, making her open her eyes slowly.

And she froze.

A small section of the ceiling retracted, leaving behind nothing but clear glass, a graveyard of stars glittering beyond in the sky.

She watched in wonder as he moved inside her, finding his own release, and a tear escaped her eye, rolling down the side of her head as he came.

She stared up, her arousal and emotions mixing together until she couldn't discern one from the other.

After a lifetime of looking at cracked ceilings and peeling paint while pieces of her were ripped from her, he had given her a ceiling of beautiful stars and slowly put the pieces back together again.

He had touched her soul.

CHAPTER 19

LYLA

She was sore, so fucking *sore* between her legs every step was making her excruciatingly aware of how deep, how thick he had been inside her. It wasn't like she hadn't had injuries to her vagina before; she had. But this soreness, though it hurt, sent warmth coursing through her veins.

She turned the coffee machine on for him, knowing he liked black coffee in the morning, and made tea for herself, wincing as she walked over the counter to get the mugs, her eyes going to see him working out in the garden, his torso gleaming with a thin sheet of sweat, his muscles bunching and releasing as he moved through some kind of martial art routine.

She ogled him as she did in the mornings while the beverages got ready, watching as he finished up and came inside, the force-field of his presence making her nerve-endings stand on attention. It wasn't like the other mornings. She had felt him now, let him in now, and there was an intimacy between them. Usually, he greeted her and went for shower.

This morning, he rounded the counter without stopping, gripped her jaw, and gave her a hard, thorough kiss that left her clutching his arms.

He pulled back, raking a dark, possessive look over her clad in his t-shirt, before coming to a stop on her lips again. His thumb moved over it, igniting little sparks under his touch. With another kiss, he stepped back and went to his coffee.

"We didn't use any protection." He pointed out as he poured in his mug.

Lyla steadied herself against the counter, watching him operate the coffee machine, and felt some of the cheer leave her. "I can't get pregnant," she told him. "After I ran away … there was too much bleeding. They had to operate on me."

He studied her quietly. "And how do you feel about that?"

His favorite question to ask her—how she felt about anything. She shrugged. "I was kind of grateful I wouldn't bring another child into that hell."

He didn't say anything for a long minute. "You know, it was your determination to save him that night that fascinated me. The way you trusted me to take him even though I could see it was killing you. It intrigued me."

Her heart thud with the memory. "How is he?"

"Good," he told her, finally giving her some answers. "He's with … a couple that loves him."

Heart full, she swallowed. "That's good. Thank you."

He didn't say anything to that, and shaking the subject off, she asked the one question that had pestered her for a while. "How did you get so much money?"

He turned to give her a look, before picking up his mug. "It's a long story."

She turned off her tea. "I have time."

His lips twitched. "When I was fifteen, I burned down the orphanage I'd been at, killing about eight adults inside. The fire was a big deal back then. Three of the adults had been members of The Syndicate."

She drew in a sharp breath, in the middle of pouring. "What did they do?"

A dark smile slashed his lips. "Made me an assassin. I had nothing against them at the time, and they knew I had no problem killing. So they sent me to hunt their targets. That made me a lot of money, which I later invested in different businesses, made even more money."

He took a sip of his drink, leaning against the counter, head titled to one side as he watched her process the information.

"Are you involved in the ... sex slaves?" she asked, hesitating, hoping he wasn't, but not understanding how she'd feel if he was.

To her great relief, he shook his head. "It's too messy and too much teamwork. I'm more of a lone hunter."

She wasn't surprised that he didn't comment about the morality of it. His sense of morality was skewed, and she knew it.

"So, when did you leave them?" she wondered, curious about how a fifteen-year-old had become such an assassin.

"Once I had access to their little secrets. About four years after I started working for them."

"Why?"

"I decided to take them down."

He stated it so casually, so simply, Lyla shook her head in disbelief that a nineteen-year-old boy could have even thought it. "You decided to take them down?"

"Yes, but they're a very old, very powerful, and very well-spread organization. It takes time to get all the pieces in place."

She marveled at that. "Wait, wouldn't they already know your name and keep an eye on you? How would you pull that off?"

He chuckled darkly. "They never had my name. I worked for them as a number, and once I was done, I disappeared for a while. All the money went into Blackthorne Group. That's not my name either, but one I took for myself."

"And Dainn?" she questioned.

"Only you know that, *flamma,*" he told her softly, and she took the moment, cherishing another little gift he'd given her. Taking a sip of her tea, she looked up at him from under her lashes, seeing the sunlight playing in his gold-green eye and glinting off his black one. Both eyes representing both men—Blackthorne and Shadow Man within him.

Which reminded her ... "Why Shadow Man? And when did you ... become him?"

He pushed one of his hands into his workout pant pockets, keeping the mug in the other, and damn he looked good. A belated tendril of heat curled in her, and she squashed it down.

"I *am* Shadow Man," he stated. "He had to come out to deal with The Syndicate. He could go, get information, do things that others couldn't. It was simple to have him. Blackthorn Group has access to current data, and I have access to the past. Between all the information I have, it's made it easier."

"And why do you want to take The Syndicate down?"

The first sign of stiffness tensed his body. His jaw worked slightly as he stared at her, and she waited, not knowing if she'd touched a nerve or if he was simply thinking. After a long minute, he put his mug down, heading toward the fridge.

"Are you sore?"

Blinking at the sudden change of topic, realizing that he wasn't going to answer her, she sighed. *Small steps*, she reminded herself. They'd made enough progress that she could let it go for now.

"I am," she answered him. "You wrecked me good last night."

His back muscles came into focus and relaxed as he rummaged in the freezer. "You should put some ice on it."

"No, it's—" The sentence died on her lips as he turned and she saw what he held in his hand.

A dildo.

An ice dildo.

A dildo made of ice, a little smaller than he was.

What in the everloving fuck?

Horrified yet intrigued, her eyes flew to him as he went to the sink and ran it under water, the crystal clear ice shining in the sunlit kitchen. Turning the tap off, he moved toward her and she scrambled back.

"Oh, no. No. That isn't going inside me," she stated firmly, looking at the dripping ice appendage in his hand. She had never had good experience with foreign objects and she had told him that. He knew she didn't like the idea of toys at all.

Unheeding, lips twitching, he put it on the counter before calmly picking her up and planting her ass on it.

"Put your feet on the slab," he instructed, pushing her knees open. "Take the t-shirt off."

Hesitating, not on-board with it, she stripped, resting her weight on her hands behind her on the counter, waiting to see what he would do.

He looked at her intently between her legs, seeing her swollen, abraded, nether lips. She'd always marked easily, and her pussy looked like it had been a battlefield.

"You had this in the freezer even though I said I didn't like foreign objects inside me?" she intuited. It wouldn't surprise her if he didn't have a regard for her boundaries. He never had, and he probably never would.

"You already know the answer to that."

Well, if he was going to push her boundaries, she was going to return the favor.

"Why are you after The Syndicate?" she pressed on, knowing that was the moment he had clocked out of the conversation and began to distract her.

Cold, chilled ice circled around her heavy breasts in a large, infinite loop, leaving her gasping. Her gasp turned into a moan when his warm tongue followed, licking up the same path, her breasts heaving under the sudden onslaught of sensation.

He made the icy cold loop again, this one tighter, closer to her aching nipples and yet so far, then followed the trail with his hot tongue, lapping the water. She lay back on the counter, her hands getting weaker, unable to support her body as she went flat on her back.

"Why are you after—?" The sentence got cut off on a strangled cry as he slapped her clit with the ice, the cold and the sensation making the little nub throb.

"Eyes."

The single command had her eyes flying open, making her realize she'd closed them at the touch. She watched with half-lidded gaze as his hand—his large, burned, hand that had killed so many people in her name she probably should've felt remorseful about it—moved the ice back to her breasts, this time straight to her nipple, circling it over and over again. Leaning over her, between her legs so she could feel his hardness nudging against her over the fabric of his pants, his warm mouth closed around the nipple while the ice went to the other one. The immediate sensation of cold and warm had a shot of fire arrow right between her thighs, making her moan as she bit her lip, her hands spearing into his dark hair. His thumb went to her lips, tracing them like he always did.

"Say my name."

With the way she knew her voice affected him, she knew he was trying to feel the sound right at the source.

"Dainn."

His eyes flared, the dark gleaming as the light one darkened.

He leaned down until his face was inches from hers, the vulnerability in her body and the heat in his gaze making her blood simmer.

"You're the only one who knows my name, *flamma*," he spoke, his words brushing her lips. "The only one who knows me as the devil I truly am. And seeing you here, willing and trusting, is the only time I come close to *feeling* something."

Lyla breathed through her nose as his words both settled and saddened her. "Will you ever love me?" she gave voice to the deepest, rawest desire of her heart.

He simply looked at her, curious from what she could sense. "What is love to you?"

The question gave Lyla pause. What was love to her? What did she actually want when she wanted to be loved? She didn't know love, had never felt it, experienced it except for the son she'd sacrificed, and that love was different. Or was it? Was all love not the same, sprouting from the same source?

"I think it's feeling safe," she told him after a long moment of thinking, a moment where he patiently waited for the answer. "Emotionally, sexually, physically, safe in every way. It's knowing you can be yourself with someone and they won't judge you. It's feeling like equals when need be and being able to give up control if need be. It's . . . feeling like you can trust someone with the darkest secrets and knowing they'll keep them safe. It's the ability to trust without thought. It's—" her voice shook as his gaze intensified "—being able to give up something important to yourself if it will help the one you love. It's putting their needs above your own. It's unconditional. That's . . . that's love for me."

He stayed still, processing everything she'd said, as though filing it is some corner of his mind to evaluate later. Her words seemed to have given him food for thought.

He suddenly pulled away and pulled back, and Lyla watched as he moved around the counter to stand at her head. He looked even larger from her upside down vantage, his shoulders broader, blocking down the light coming from the windows behind him. His shadow fell over her entire naked body and she reveled in it, waiting to see what he was going to do next. The man constantly surprised her in so many ways.

"What does love mean for you?" she asked, curious and cautious.

His head dipped down, pressing a soft, almost gentle kiss to her lips, the upside down position of their mouths making it an experience she'd not experienced before. An inch away after kissing her, he spoke against her mouth. "If there was any love in this world of mine, Lyla, it would be you."

Her heart stopped.

"Dainn," she whispered, knowing this wasn't something he would just say casually, knowing it meant something.

"I am darkness." He kissed her softly. "I live it, I breathe it, I am it. There is no redemption, no emotion, nothing for me. Nothing but you. You're the moon to my dark night, *flamma.* You're the only thing in this black sky that can thrive when I swallow everything else whole. The stars don't exist in this space. Just you and I. You need me to glow and I need you to exist. It's simple as that."

Tears were pooling in her eyes. For being an emotionless bastard sometimes, this man said the most beautiful things.

"That was beautiful," she told him so, a warm glow filling her. The way he saw her was beautiful, the way he was with her was beautiful.

He dipped his mouth to her ear, placing the ice toy she'd forgotten about at her thigh. "Now let me ice that sore pussy."

Before she could even blink at the sudden switch in conversation, the ice dildo was on her pussy.

"Fuck, that's cold!" she exclaimed, trying to move up and away from it when something hard hit her head. She tilted her neck and saw his hard, veiny, pierced cock level with her mouth, the angle making it appear even more massive.

Even sore and exhausted, her walls clenched. The ice rubbed her gently, from her lips to her clit, up and down, melting from the heat of her skin and lubricating her with more than her juices. She wondered how his hand wasn't burning from holding it like that for so long, and realized given his proclivities for fire maybe he didn't entirely mind the sensation.

"Careful," she warned him, not sure if it was for his hand or her pussy or her mouth, but saw him gave her a small twitch of his lips.

"Relax for me," he cajoled, and she relaxed, both her jaw and her muscles.

And then, from both ends, he entered her.

Slowly.

The cold, ice dildo penetrated her from one end, the chill making her want to freeze but the sensation unlike any she'd ever experienced in her entire sexual life. The hot, heavy cock penetrated her from the other end, slowly taking her mouth so as not to injure her with his size or the metal. The cold and the hot, both burning her from both ends, was such an intense, otherworldly experience she couldn't even process what was happening within her body. Her nipples were stiff and aching, her breasts heavy and needing attention, her skin breaking out in goosebumps and spine arching to keep up with all the mixed signals her brain was sending to her flesh.

He pulled out both himself and the ice at the same time, making her draw a huge breath before she was impaled again, same time, both sides. The groan in her throat got trapped, muffled around his cock, his ladder piercings rubbing the roof of her mouth in a way that made saliva pool in her mouth. The ice on the other hand kept moving in and out of her rapidly, the heat of her walls both melting it and molding around it.

The motion from both ends kept her in place, and she grabbed his hips to anchor herself, right as he leaned over the counter and her. His mouth, his hot, wet mouth, fell upon her cold clit, and Lyla froze, on the brink of an orgasm she could almost touch within her reach, an orgasm that would felt so massive she knew it would end her. Her breathing became harsher, the burn from both cocks inside her spreading under her skin, her toes curling, her legs moving restlessly to find some kind of purchase, her nails digging into his ass as he alternated between flicking and sucking her clit, the ice dildo melting rapidly but still penetrating her as she sucked on him, determined to make him cum with her.

It built and built and built until she reached the crescendo, a scream building in her chest as stars burst behind her eyelids, his mouth and the dildo leaving her, and she came.

She *came.*

All over the counter.

The biggest, most sensational orgasm of her life.

Her body shook, her legs jerking as the pleasure mounting her exploded for minutes and hours and she honestly didn't know how long.

Fuck.

It subsided slowly, making her open her eyes and realize her mouth was empty and he was back around the counter, just watching her as she gradually came down.

Reborn. She felt reborn.

Her belief system broken and assimilated again.

The two things she'd hated the most—oral and toys—had given her the most exquisite orgasm of her life. It had been dirty, vulgar and so messy, it should've made her feel used. She felt used but she felt cherished, safe, and pleasured—used in a way that left her feeling sappy instead of shameful.

She sat up on the counter, her heart feeling tender, overflowing with an unnamed emotion for this man who was building her back up, one broken piece at a time.

"Come here." She let her jittery legs dangle down, opening her arms up to him.

He shook his head. "That wasn't for me."

It was for her. After being taken and taken and taken from, she was being given.

Fuck, he was undoing her.

"Come here," she invited him again, and this time he did, walking to her with the lithe grace of a wild panther. As soon as he was within reach, she wrapped her arms around him, nuzzling his chest, pressing her ear to his chest to remind herself that his heart did beat too.

She didn't take him in, and he didn't enter her, but he did hold her tightly and let her take whatever she needed from him.

His chest rumbled as he spoke to her head. "Still hate toys?"

"Not with you." She rubbed her nose over his heart.

His hand came to her hair, pulling her head back, as he looked down at her intently. "There will never be anyone else."

"Even if I choose another?" she asked, just to provoke him.

His hand on her head flexed, the possession in his eyes so intense it sent her heart fluttering.

"If you ever choose another, make sure you kill me first. Because I—" he bent to whisper against her lips "—will annihilate the fucking *world* before I let you go."

There was something truly messed up with her because instead of scaring her, it just made her feel more cherished. She loved that. She loved that she meant enough to him.

Feeling claimed, feeling chosen, Lyla held the man she realized ticked almost every box of love for her.

CHAPTER 20

HIM

She was ready.

He watched as she moved around the kitchen, immensely enjoying the way his t-shirt fell over her petite frame, almost drowning her to her knees. She had begun to make this space her own, and he liked that.

For weeks, they had stayed here. For weeks, almost two months since the night he drove inside her, tasting the sweetness of her cries on his tongue and seeing the burst of sparks across his vision, he had become addicted. Her sounds had different flavors of sweetness too—and nothing had been more delicious than every time he took her to the stars and back.

"Do you think you can handle going back to the city?" he asked, testing her, waiting to see her reaction.

She stiffened with her back to him, her arms freezing on the door of the refrigerator. "Do I have to?" Her voice had a tremor in it. Sweet but oddly sour too. He didn't like when she spoke in pain or fear.

"Come here."

Without hesitation, she turned and came to him, sitting down on his lap. He was pleased. For two months, she had learned to trust him, learned to let go, and she had received only pleasure for it. He'd made it his life's mission to replace her horrors with happiness, the demons in her past with the devil in her present. He wanted her to remain happy. When she was, his world was different. Her eyes sparkled, her hair was shinier, her voice tasted sweeter, the sounds she made hit him in the chest. He wasn't just addicted to her now; he was addicted to her when she was happy, her laughter a new sound to add to the list of his obsessions. It was such an odd sound, not one he was very familiar with and not one he'd particularly thought would come from her, but once it had, he wanted more. Her breathy sighs, her soft moans, her shattering screams—he wanted them all. The way she said his name, the way she tested his boundaries, the way she looked at him—he was a man crazed for those little things.

He looked down at her face, her beautiful face that glowed with health and life, her hair slightly longer and going back to its original waviness of a flame, her bright green eyes so expressive he still wondered how one person could hold so much emotion inside them.

They were perfect, she and him—her soul full of emotion and light and his of void and dark. And somehow, even with his void and his dark, she didn't lose her innate ability to emote, to shine, to warm. She felt like the fire he had needed in the midst of winter on the streets, when he'd been freezing and there had been nothing to warm him. That's what his life had been like, endless winter with no warmth in sight, and somehow he had accepted the frost into himself. And she, that night he had been about to deliver a death, had instead delivered life in his hands, trusting him with her most precious possession.

Nobody had ever trusted him, never with anything precious, and the feeling had become heady. Trust was power, the power to make or break someone. And in that moment, having never tasted that kind of emotional power before, he had been stunned.

He liked her trust, he wanted her trust. He wanted to break her and rebuild her, and he wanted her trust to let him do all those things. She didn't know this, but she had been his purpose for six years, all his plans, all his actions, everything centered around her.

She was the sun in the endless dark abyss of the universe, a ball of fire so bright she made everything revolve around herself without even trying, and anything that didn't was lost to float away and die. And he? He was the endless, dark abyss they died in, the one that surrounded her, the one that let her blaze.

He watched as wriggled a little in his lap, sending blood rushing to his cock. The fucker was addicted to her pussy too. Fucking her the first time had been like fucking for the first time. He hadn't expected the sensations of her tight pussy gripping him to feel so heightened when he'd gotten the piercings. Even now, it took him a moment to fully seat himself inside her and he had been consistently taking her for weeks.

"Stop," he held her hip still, knowing she was trying to distract him.

She didn't stop.

Without a word, he stood and pushed her over the counter, giving her ass a loud smack. Another thing he'd learned about her? She loved being spanked. The first time he'd spanked her had been a throwaway gesture as he'd passed her in the closet. He hadn't been thinking about doing it, but her ass had looked good in her jeans and he'd just impulsively done it.

She'd yelped and turned around, and the expression on her face had said everything.

So, he'd done it again.

She had bitten her lush lower lip, her eyes hungry.

So, right there in the closet, he had turned her over his knee and spanked her until she'd been a writhing mess, crying and begging him to take her, and take her he had, right in front of the mirror, holding her up with his arms, her legs up over his forearms locking her open, making her see how small she had looked with his huge, pierced cock hammering into her. She had come so many times that time she had ultimately passed out.

Now, she looked over her shoulder at him, giving him *the* look he'd come to understand very well. If he was addicted to her, she was addicted to him too. And that's how he knew she was ready.

"I asked you a question," he reminded her, and she wriggled her hips back into him, rubbing against the tent in his pants, and *fuck* if he didn't want to rip into her.

"I don't want to leave home," she told him, and something tightened in his chest.

Home.

She'd begun to think of this as home. He was very, very pleased.

"You can't hide forever, *flamma.*"

"Watch me."

The defiance in her tone amused him. He gave her delectable ass another smack, watching it ripple under his palm, the red print darkening on her skin.

"If we don't go back, how will you see the bald man?"

She stilled, drawing a sharp breath in. He watched as she turned her neck, her expressive eyes locking with his. Though she had been coping, her sessions with Dr. Manson doing her a world of good, he knew she pushed a lot of what she had gone through under the rug, pretending to start anew, and while he had no problem with her healing however she had to, he did have a problem with the breakdowns that sneaked up on her unannounced.

In the last two months, he had seen her collapse over tea, over seeing a naked woman with him, over not being able to go into the village because she was scared of going out of the house, over her fear of not being talkative enough to hold a conversation. Little things, so many things, that went through her mind and made her feel lesser, all coming from a place of low self-worth and fear of never being enough. With the life she'd had, no one could blame her but fuck if he didn't want her to realize and accept just how truly powerful she was, had always been. In a war, the one who had the most effective weapons was the mightier, and she, even without knowing, had some of the most powerful weapons in the world willing to go to any lengths for her. He was just on the top of that list, so if it meant killing the main monster responsible for recent traumas, then so be it.

Hector, once Alpha Villanova's right-hand man, now a Syndicate lapdog, was the lowest of lowlives. While Dainn didn't have any room to judge as a killer himself, Hector was a breed of his own. He had fucked children, raped and strangled innocent women, and murdered one of Lyla's old friend, one who had escaped and become Alpha's sister-in-law. Dainn, as psychotic as he was, drew the line at kids, not because of morality bur because they were helpless, powerless, and it made those who preyed on them cowards who couldn't face a grown adult.

Dainn had been tracking Hector since the day he'd taken Lyla, terrorizing him until the other man peed his pants and ran away to hide like the spineless coward that he was. He had resurfaced, and this time, the Shadow Man would pay him a visit.

"You know where he is?" she asked, rage bleaching into her words.

"Better, *flamma*," he palmed her ass softly. "I have him strung up in a very good place. He's bleeding out, one drop at a time as I play with your pussy." She spread her legs for his fingers, wet for him already as she always was.

"Is he hurting?" she asked, her voice trembling.

"More than you ever hurt," he promised and saw her spine relax. *Good.*

"I want to see that," she said softly to the counter. "I want to see him bleed. When do we go?"

Dainn heard her vengeful words, and slowly rubbed her back in a gesture he knew soothed her. Yeah, she was ready, at least for the first step.

CHAPTER 21

LYLA

She wasn't ready to leave the house. Over the weeks, it had become a haven, the only home she had ever known, the only heaven in her life of hell. And she wasn't ready to let it go, unsure if she would ever return, the part of her that still questioned herself constantly wondering if he would leave her in the city. She would miss the house, the deck, the routine. She would miss cooking and being herself, meeting Dr. Manson everyday and taking walks around the garden with Bessie. She would miss it all.

She shook her head and snapped the hair tie she'd put around her wrist. Dr. Manson had suggested tying a hair tie around her wrist and snapping it whenever a bad, baseless thought entered her mind. When she'd looked up an article on the same, it said that it trained the brain to feel punished for bad thoughts and so eventually, it became more manageable.

It had been a few weeks and she could attest that it did work for her. Training her brain into different thought patterns was something she had been working on actively. Some things she did on her own, like the hair tie, like the daily tasks, like writing something good about every day. Some things she needed help with, and the man who was a nightmare to so many people helped her.

Like she had told him how going into the bathtub reminded her of all the times she had tried to drown herself under the water, and he had simply started drawing her a bath every night. He picked her up and carried her in arms, sitting down on one end and making her sit on him, with her back to his front and him inside her, not moving, not fucking, just still, so she began to associate the tub and baths with him.

Another time, she'd told him about how in the past having her asshole touched made her feel sick and dirty, how the thought of it still made her stomach turn. And he, deviant, dominant he, had tied her ankles to her wrists until she was obscenely exposed, and put a vibrator on her clit, his cock in her pussy, and his thumb in her rosebud until she had forgotten it had even been there, lost in the sensations. The next morning, before he left, he had turned her over the couch and spanked her ass, lubing her up with her own juices, and put a small plug in her backside, telling her not to take it out, not to touch herself, not to do a thing to it until he returned. The entire day, the weight of the object in one hole and the emptiness of the object in another had messed with her nerves until she had been on the deck, naked, her legs spread over the arms of the chair just to let the cool breeze give her overheated skin some relief. That was how he'd found her, and he'd caged her on the chair, leaning over, and pushed himself inside her, double penetrating her in a way that had made her mindless with sensations, her screams echoing over the mountains until she passed out.

But it wasn't just her sexual hang-ups he was helping her work through. It was emotional too.

She'd confessed to him how insecure she felt, how she feared he would leave her one day and she didn't know if she could handle that. The next morning, he had taken her to the closet, and stood behind her. Brining up his hands, he had told her to close her eyes. She had, and immediately something cold, metallic had touched the skin around her neck, making her breath hitch. She had opened her eyes to see a gold, thin choker around her neck, the metal warming to her body temperature.

"Just like your hair tie," he'd murmured with his lips against her neck. "When you feel that insecurity, touch this, remind yourself who claimed you, remind yourself of the last six years and how I never let you go once, and ask yourself if you ever think I'd let you go now. The world could tilt on its axis, *flamma,* and I'd still be the most certain thing in your life." A soft kiss. "You're the oxygen that feeds my flames—without you, my existence is questionable."

She touched the gold chain around her neck as he locked the door, taking her toward the helicopter in the early morning light. As she walked to the waiting ride, a thrill of excitement shot up her spine. She'd been fascinated with the thing since she had seen it on her first morning. She got to the side of the black helicopter and she turned around to look at the house, a gray and black sleek marvel of architecture half on the cliff and a little under.

Looking at the house, she remembered the day she'd confessed in the dark of the night that she didn't know where she would go if she ever had to be alone, that she had nothing on the outside. He had listened intently with his arms around her, and the next day, he'd taken her to the safe in the study.

"Sit," he told her, and she took a seat. He sat down next to her, turning his whole body toward her, handing her a manila envelope.

"What's this?" she asked, curious about the content as she pulled it out. She looked over a bunch of legal jargon, most of it flying over her head, and turned questioning eyes to him.

He pointed at the first document. "That is the deed to this house. It's in your name—Lyla Blackthorne—and it's all yours."

Stunned, she looked down at the paper again, and sure enough the words 'property' and 'belong' and her name, her new name, were there. While she processed it, the enormity of it, he continued. "I had this house built for you. You'll always have a place to go that is only yours."

Tears welled up in her eyes as she clutched the document to her chest, the gesture, the thought, more important than he'd ever know.

He picked up a second document, his hypnotic dual light and dark eyes steady on hers. "This—" he handed her the second document "—is a marriage license, officially declaring you Mrs. Blackthorne. So you own everything I own, and you can go anywhere in the world and have a name."

Fuck.

"But we didn't get married," she pointed out, not understanding how he'd gotten it done.

"In the eyes of the law, we did." The statement was enough in itself. It hadn't been lawful whatever he'd done to make it possible, but he'd done that.

He had given her a home and a name, a place and a person to belong, space to learn who she was and what her individuality was, her likes and dislikes, her hopes and inhibitions. He had given her the ability to dream.

Without a word, she crashed her lips into his, thanking him the only way she could, by pouring everything she was feeling into that one kiss, letting him understand what it meant to her. He gripped her jaw like he always did, his tongue twining with hers, and accepted what she gave, demanding more, demanding everything, merging them so completely until she didn't know where she ended and where he began.

After long, long minutes of kissing, she pulled back, her lips swollen, her eyes shining. "I think I'm in love with you."

He brushed his nose against hers, his eyes soft on her. "I know that you are."

And though he didn't say he loved her back, though she didn't know if he felt it, it was enough. Everything he had been for years, everything he had been for weeks, everything he had done to empower her, it was enough.

He had given her many gifts but his biggest, most beautiful had been freedom. What she'd thought of as a prison in the beginning had instead been a safe space for her to be, to explore herself, to live without fear.

She was *free.*

She was *fearless.*

She was *flying.*

And it was all because of him.

And that was more than enough.

The feel of his hand on her back brought her back to the present as he picked her up and put her in. She sat still as he strapped her in, her heart beating in happy rhythms as she watched him, his dark hair, his permanent scruff, his mismatched, hypnotic, devilish eyes. He gripped her jaw and gave her a hard, quick kiss.

"You love me," he stated, as he had begun stating every day since she'd told him.

"I love you," she confirmed, brushing her nose against his.

He kissed her again and pulled back, shutting the door at her side. She saw him walk lithely to the pilot's side and climb in with an agility that belied how often he'd done this. He shut his door and strapped himself in, and she watched with absorption as he began to push some buttons that made no sense to her. He put on his headgear and indicated to hers, and she put it on, eager to see what happened next.

After he did some checks, he pushed a button that sent vibrations running through her body as the blades of the helicopter started to move. Gripping the edges of her seat, heart pounding, her stomach dropped as the ground slowly began to move lower. They dipped forward slightly before steadying, hovering, and she absorbed the entire vista of the mountains, the cliffs, the sea, the beach, the house, spread out below for her to feast her eyes upon.

"Wow," she breathed out, still amazed that she could see something like this when a few months ago all she'd expected out of life had been a clean end. She had changed since then, evolved, grown. Like a tree that had been cut and ravaged and pulled until nothing remained for the eye to see. He hadn't seen the ripped roots, the bleeding stump, the utter destruction. No, he had seen life. He had taken the single root, put it in a controlled, safe environment, and fed it sunlight and water and affection in his own way until a new shoot had emerged, new roots had planted, new flowers had bloomed.

Eyes glued to the vista below as they got higher and higher, she felt her stomach twist with every vibration and glide of the helicopter. She turned to see him, watching the little smile on his lips as he took them across the mountains inland toward the city—Gladestone.

He had told her about it one day when she'd asked about where she had been, where the complex had been. He'd told her about Gladestone, a city that emerged in the 1800s, known for its mining and textile industrial prowess. It was a fast-paced city, a place where people didn't sleep and crime didn't stop. It was one of the key locations for The Syndicate's operations, something she'd learned from him later. That was what had brought him to Gladestone all those years ago in the first place. It was a dark, polluted settlement of mostly people who had something or the other to do with the underworld—be in humans, organs, animals, murderers, or more.

After about half an hour of flying, she got to see the first of the tall factory chimneys from a distance.

"That's Gladestone's outskirts," he told her, his voice loud and crackling with static in her headphones. Factories after factories passed under her, the view so drastically different from the one she'd seen around home.

Home.

It still sent disbelief coursing through her when she said that.

The cityscape come across the view after a few minutes, the factories and warehouses falling away to show cleaner, taller buildings. The first glimmer of the black hole opened in her mind in months watching the city that had destroyed her.

"Where's the Club District?" she shouted over the mouthpiece.

He pointed right. "Over there. You used to live farther in that direction."

She touched her choker, taking a deep breath, and snapped her hair tie again, rooting herself in the present. It was fine. She was fine. She was not the same girl who had given in to the black hole. She was new and she would be fine.

Dainn circled a tall building, one of the tallest in the skylines, and she saw a helipad on top of the roof. "We're going down."

She gave a thumbs up sign, and held onto her straps, her stomach whooping as they descended. She regulated her breathing, knowing it would take some getting used to for this to feel normal, and they touched the roof.

Within moments, once the helicopter was set, he pushed more buttons and turned it off, the blades slowing down until they stopped.

Unbuckling himself, he jumped down from the pilot's cockpit and came around to her, getting her out and on the roof in record time.

Her knees shook but she stood with his support, feeling the wind on her face, the sun on her skin, the view—although beautiful in its own way—marred by her memories. She hated this city and hated its people.

"Mr. Blackthorne, welcome."

The voice from a woman on the side made her turn. A pretty woman in some kind of a uniform led them toward an elevator.

"Thank you, Fiona." He pasted a charming smile on his face and took her hand. "I hope you have our suite ready? My wife is tired from the trip."

For the first time, she saw why people fell for his facade without seeing who he was underneath. The woman ate it up, and to be honest, so did she, especially the 'wife' part.

"Of course, Mr. Blackthorne." The woman pressed a keycard to a fancy, fancy elevator. "Should I tell *Moonflame* to expect you tonight?"

"Yes, please. Thank you, Fiona."

The elevator doors closed and Lyla watched in fascination as his smile dropped, his usual, neutral expression back on his face, his eyes hidden behind the dark shades he had worn. He took his phone out from his suit pocket, the other holding hers, and operated it with one hand.

And she liked that. She liked that he was real with her, just as he was, no pretenses.

"Dainn," she tugged his hand.

"Hmm?"

"*Moonflame?*"

He paused, looking at her, knowing she was asking him about the sex club they had met in once years ago, a sex club that had been a nightmare for her.

"Why are you going there tonight?"

He pocketed his phone, turning to her. "*We* are going there tonight. I bought the club after that night in the maze. Changed things up. We are going because I want you to experience what an actual sex club is like."

She looked at his chest exposed by his unbuttoned shirt. "Are you . . . do you force people there?"

"Not if they don't want to be forced."

People wanted to be forced? What the fuck?

She felt his breath on her cheek. "Close your eyes."

Her eyes shuttered immediately.

"Now imagine me," his voice wrote seduction on her skin. "Imagine me pushing you down and you struggling to get away. Deep down, you know I wouldn't hurt you, but this is a game, and so we pretend. I pretend and chase you, you pretend and run. I catch you—" her breath hitched as his hands skimmed over her sides "—and push you face down into the bed. You pretend to struggle, you want to get away from me, but I tie you up, you can't move. So you scream."

His hand suddenly covered her mouth, his voice in her ear as he came behind her. "I muffle your screams, take my hand lower, choke you until you stop."

Memories collided with the fantasy inside her, her body trembling as he kept weaving the words over her. "So you stop screaming, stop struggling. And then I push my cock inside your tight little cunt—" his hand cupped her over her jeans "—and if you make one noise, I'll choke you."

She could hear her loud breathing, almost pants at the visual he created in her mind.

"Would you want this fantasy?"

Before she could say another word, the elevator doors opened and so did her eyes, flying to see the three people staring at her with wide eyes. She could imagine what they looked like—a small woman with a large man looming behind her, his hand over her mouth and between her legs.

The said hand gave her a little squeeze before he let go, twining their fingers together again and taking her with him.

He was rewriting her sexual experiences, and she trusted him to do it.

"With you, I would," she told him like always.

"There would never be anyone else," he promised as always.

CHAPTER 22

LYLA

At dusk, dainn took her arm and led her to the parking lot of the hotel they were staying at. He'd rented the suite out on a permanent basis since the hotel was both upscale and close to the Club District, the place where he'd mainly needed to be when he was in town. Since he was a semipermanent resident, the hotel had given him a permanent parking spot, the one where he led her to, a sleek black car waiting for them.

She didn't know what the car was or the company but it looked fast, and she wasn't surprised. Between his flying and driving, she'd understood he liked the rush.

Getting into the low, very low car, the interior of it unsurprisingly black too, she strapped herself in and they pulled out.

"Why Blackthorne?" she mused. "Out of all the names you could have picked, why that?"

A side of his mouth twitched. "It was the name of the first man I killed. He was a rich, pompous asshole, and since that's who I was going to pretend to be, why not?"

Lyla drew in a sharp breath. "How old were you?"

"Six." The little smile on his face was disturbing. It disturbed her even more that she wasn't disturbed. Shouldn't she have been more horrified, more repulsed than sleep with a killer so willingly? Perhaps. Maybe she would have been in an alternative reality where she was normal.

"And why did you kill him?" she kept on, ignoring the thoughts in her head.

He slid her a glance. "He took something from me."

Something in his tone felt like a door shut. She recognized the tone enough, having been subjected to it a few times in the last two months. Usually, he answered whatever questions she had, let her test as many boundaries as she wanted. But some, he closed up on. And as understanding as she wanted to be, it frustrated her because he knew everything about her, had witnessed her most humiliating moments, and she didn't have the same privilege when it came to him. She knew his personality, knew who he was, but his past was a vault she hadn't been given access to yet.

As he swerved around the city, maneuvering the car expertly, she slid him a look. He was dressed up, in a dark suit without the tie, his hair pushed back from the lines of his face, his mismatched eyes dangerous. She was dressed up herself, in a champagne-colored gown with a side split and strings on her shoulders, her hair slightly longer and open in their waves, her lips painted a soft blush she knew he was obsessed with.

She was apprehensive about both being in the city and going to *Moonflame*. Regardless of what he said, the memory of being tied up and pushed in a maze, of feeling helpless and hunted, was acute in her mind. She didn't know how he could override all that.

Dr. Manson's words came to her.

'Open yourself up to new experiences. Trusting your partner is utmost for any relationship. Has he given you a reason not to trust him?'

No. No, he hadn't.

Reminding herself of that, touching the gold choker on her neck, she watched the city pass by as they pulled into a familiar parking lot. *Moonflame* was one of the Club District buildings, a simple two-story gray structure that nobody would have given a second look at, not with all the flashy signs everywhere else. A simple black plaque hung on the wooden door, nothing but the logo of an orb on fire. She assumed it was the literal moon on flame.

Parking the car, he turned to face her. "I'll be with you the whole time."

She nodded.

Giving her a soft kiss, he exited, coming around to her side and taking her hand. He put his gloved hand on her back, guiding her to the main door.

Dainn knocked sharply on the door three times with his gloved knuckles, and a man opened the door, letting them into a narrow corridor. The corridor opened in an open hall, and Lyla huddled into his side instinctively as deja-vu flooded her. He held her close, walking into the lounge area done in wooden and reds, and if she didn't see a few people in different stages of copulation here and there, she wouldn't have thought it was a sex club at all. It had changed a lot from the last time she had been there.

Dainn led her through the lounge toward the back where there was another door, the one that had led to the maze room, and her heart began to stutter, her feet stumbling.

His hold on her waist tightened, but he continued to lead her.

The door opened, and instead of the maze, there were sets of stairs.

Curious, surprised, she followed as he led her up some stairs to the right, one that opened into a small room painted dark red, with nothing but a couch looking at a large glass wall looking into an auditorium style room, no sign of the maze.

Her lips parted.

A brunette woman was strung up, suspended by a rope hanging from the ceiling, her toes touching the ground, a blindfold over her eyes, her body completely naked.

Lyla looked over and saw at least ten other glass rooms looking down on the scene, the glasses tinted lightly enough to only show silhouettes. She could see the silhouettes of two women playing with each other in the window opposite hers. In another, a woman was down on her knees and sucking a man's cock. In another, two women and two men were moving.

It was *debauchery*, nothing like the clubs she'd ever seen.

She took a step closer to the glass as two men, completely dressed, joined the suspended woman in the middle of the auditorium. The contrast between them, the men fully clothed and her fully on display, sent a wisp of arousal curling through her.

The auditorium was different, the vibe was different. It didn't feel invasive, not like it had the last time.

She felt him stand behind her, his gloved finger tracing her collarbones as her breaths turned ragged. "Do you like what I've done with this?"

Lyla bit her lip, nodding. "Yes."

"And you like the scene?"

Lyla looked down at the scene, both men sucking on both the suspended woman's nipples, drawing in so deep she could see their cheeks hollow. They weren't touching the woman anywhere else, and she hung on, moaning, her legs thrashing to find purchase. The idea that she was blindfolded but being watched by so many did something to her.

"She wants to be there, right?" The question was important to her.

"Everyone here wants to be here."

Good. That was good.

"Would you let anyone see me like that?" she asked, curious about how his possessiveness could handle that.

His dark chuckle washed over her. "I could fuck you raw with the whole world watching, Lyla. Watching from afar, knowing they couldn't have you, couldn't even touch you, that you were all mine to play with as I pleased. But I wouldn't let you come. That is for *my* eyes only."

The possession of his words slithered through her body, stoking the heat higher.

"I . . . I don't know what I think of that," she muttered, her eyes on the scene below. She had hated being on display. What she had with him was just theirs, just between them, and the idea of showing it out didn't appeal to her.

His lips landed on her neck. "But you like watching?"

His question made sense to her. "Yes."

She felt his warm breath against the side of her neck. "In that case, *flamma,* keep watching."

She did.

She watched as people in the other glass rooms, or rather their silhouettes, engaged in different sexual activities. She wondered, watching them, what they could see when they looked at her glass—just his silhouette as his body covered hers or a small woman with a larger man behind her back? Even not knowing, the idea was thrilling. Letting her eyes drift, she saw as the woman in the auditorium-like room was sandwiched between the two men, picked up by the one at her front while the one at her back unzipped himself.

Knowing what she knew was going to happen, she still held her breath as he entered her backside, the woman moaning so loudly it sent shivers over her body.

Lyla felt the skirt of her dress going over her hips, the man behind her pulling her panties to the side, his fingers finding her drenched already as she breathed rapidly. She felt something metallic swirl around her opening, and her body automatically stiffened.

"Shh," he settled her. "Keep watching."

She focused on the sight below. Man A set himself entirely within the woman's ass, just as Lyla felt the metal bullet Dainn had used before on her slip inside hers. The woman below moaned again as Man B unzipped himself and pushed inside her from the front, stuffing her to the maximum.

The bullet settled within her, Lyla felt the head of his cock at her opening, and leaned into the glass, canting her hips to give him better access. Lodged at the opening for a second, she watched the men below begin to slowly fuck the hanging woman as Lyla herself got impaled. Her breath hitched at the tightness of the penetration, the fact that he still needed to slip into her carefully after all this time making her heart race faster.

Within seconds, she was double downed, as close to a double penetration as she could be with this man, and knowing he would never let another near her, she let go of any inhibitions.

A loud noise escaped her at the tightness; her eyes fluttering close as she felt him go deep in, the metal on his cock rubbing against her clenching walls in a way that had become familiar but no less exquisite now.

"You hated being on display, didn't you?" The words against her neck made her shiver, goosebumps scattering over her arms.

She had, and this wasn't really her being on display per se but in a way she was too because the glass didn't hide her and her noises certainly didn't. It made her realize that yet again, he had barreled through something she had previously despised, replacing the act with an unforgettable, incredible memory instead in its place.

She let one of her hands curl around his neck, felt him deep inside her, and turned her neck, their faces inches apart. "What I had before wasn't sex. It was cruelty and it was cold. Being used, being displayed, being touched, everything was humiliating. I didn't know it could be different, that I could feel different, until you. You showed me sex was deeper. It's a way to connect to someone you care about. You breathed life back into me, and at this point, I—" she rotated her hips, their lips inches apart, seeing the affect her words had on him "—trust you to do whatever you want with me, knowing I will always be safe in the end."

His lips slanted over hers, hard, rough, his tongue pushing into her mouth as he moved inside her, her noises drowning against him.

"So," he asked, pulling back, "you would trust me if I took you down into a room full of people and left you there naked?"

Her breath hitched at the thought, dread filling her but she nodded. "Yes."

"And if I invited people here to watch this, you'd trust me?"

"Yes."

"And if I slipped something in your drink, still?"

She looked deep into his eyes, knowing he knew that being drugged was a worse memory for her. She swallowed but nodded.

"Fuck, Lyla," he groaned, thrusting so hard inside her she almost blacked out. "Nothing gets me like your trust. *Nothing*."

"I trust you," she breathed, and felt his response in a full body shudder, one that seeped into her as he proceeded to undo her. She turned back to the glass, watching the debauchery all around her, and for the first time in a long time, felt happy about being owned.

CHAPTER 23

HIM

She slept like the dead, exhausted after the sexual wringer he'd put her body through at *Moonflame.* She had surprised him. Out of all of her inhibitions, being on display had been the one that she'd hated the most for understandable reasons. But somehow, she trusted him to take care of her, and that more than anything made him feel like the most powerful of all. Her had her love, he had her trust, and that was how he knew it was time.

Looking down at the tablet, he looked at the gallery of photos he'd taken through the years, and sighed. Locking the tablet, he put it on the side table and lay down, his arm going around her small frame.

She curled back into him unconsciously, her lips moving in a mumble he couldn't hear, and he felt something tighten in his chest. Holding her, sleeping next to her, being with her, it had changed him, opened him up to possibilities and ideas, and the range of emotions he still didn't feel to the fullest extent but one he knew about.

Giving her a squeeze, he pressed a soft kiss to her head, before getting out of the bed. Knowing she'd sleep through the night—she always did after an intense fucking—he dressed in his dark athletic wear, put his phone in his pocket just in case she woke up and needed him, and quietly went to the window.

One of the reasons he stayed in this room was because of the emergency access ladder that was right outside his window. He could use it and go down without getting on any cameras inside the hotel. It also gave him the additional thrill of stymieing any watching eyes.

To the world, Blackthorne was asleep in the bed with his beautiful wife. It was time for the Shadow Man to walk.

Out the window and down the ladder, he jumped into the side alley, slowly walking down the street to the warehouse they had kept her locked up in. Poetic justice or simple vengeance, he didn't know, but he was keeping both Hector and the second guy there. She had been right under his nose and he'd been looking everywhere else.

Six months. They had kept her in chains and broken down the last remaining pieces of her, to the point she had been driven to the arms of death when she'd gotten out. The first week she had been back at home, she had barely left her room, barely eaten, barely talked. It had taken her days to slowly unfurl, open up, and let him in. Days where his connection with her over the years hadn't meant a thing because she had been too depressed.

Enjoying the dark of the night as he made his way through, he realized this was probably the one thing he was going to enjoy the most.

The warehouse they had kept her in came into view and he slipped inside. The long, industrial space was empty, just like he wanted it to be for anyone who came stumbling. Making his way through the side, he went to the back, to the tiny hellhole of a room she had been put in, the ceiling she had stared up at day after day. He had seen every single video they had sent out, seen the way her eyes had slowly died, her body had given up, her mind had left. He had seen, and if there was one thing on this planet that could make him go berserk, it was that. He had killed more people in those six months than he had in the last decade, asking, interrogating, disposing.

The Syndicate was fucking shaking in their boots at that point. Out of the five members they had at the top of the pyramid, he had already finished off three, with only two remaining and both of them in the wind, hiding like the snakes they were until he was done.

Oh, he wasn't done.

He pushed open the door to the little room, and entered, the hood drawn over his face.

The pungent scent of blood, urine and decay filled his nose. He was glad that his olfactory senses weren't as sharp.

Hector was strung up, hanging from the ceiling much like the woman in *Moonflame* had been. The difference? He was bleeding from little cuts and he wasn't about to get any pleasure. Of the three men, Hector had been the one who broke her the most, the one who came to her the most and killed little parts of her every time. And he was the one who put the camera in the room, to make sure Dainn could live every moment with her. That was how he'd seen her rip the roses he'd given her, how he'd seen her hack into her beautiful, long hair until it was all on the floor.

His chest tightened with the memory. He remembered watching that, breathing through his nose as his glass of water had cracked in his hand, just glad that she was alive and breathing. As long as she kept breathing, he would find her. As long as she kept breathing, he would bring her back. As long as she kept breathing, he would stay in control.

A man with nothing to lose was the most dangerous creature on this earth. And as long as she breathed, he had something to lose, something to long, something to live for.

He left Hector as he was, unconscious and hanging, and turned to the other guy, one tied to a chair and not bleeding. Yet.

"Rise and shine," he said, throwing the little cabinet on the side on the floor.

Both monsters jerked awake from the bang.

Hector's eyes widened with terror, the other guy swallowed.

"P . . .please," the second guy stuttered. "Let me go. I didn't do anything. I swear. I can get you whatever you want. Let me go."

Dainn simply sat down on the upturned cabinet, his hands hanging loosely, elbows resting on his knees, his lighter in his gloved hands. He didn't wear the gloves because he didn't like people seeing his burned hands—from an accidental fire when he was younger. No, that he didn't give a shit about. It was because hands touched things, and he didn't like other people's essence on him. They also helped his fingerprints not land on things and that was useful, especially since Blackthorne Group was a well-oiled machine. But mainly, it was because of the essence. The only essence he liked on his naked hands was hers. Just hers.

"What did you think was going to happen?" he asked casually, enjoying the fear in his eyes. "When you raped her, multiple times, on camera, knowing I was going to watch, hmm?"

He stood up, walking around to the back, seeing how both of them turned their necks to keep him in sight. It was useless. He knew how to use shadows, and that's what he did, merging into them until they couldn't see him, only hear his voice, amping up their terror.

"You invited the devil to play, don't beg for mercy when he shows up."

The second guy whimpered, the sound grating on his nerves. His whimper was like chalk on board, making him want to snap it. When she whimpered, sometimes in pleasure, sometimes in pain, it made him want to wrap her in his arms and keep her to himself.

Hector spoke, breaking the silence. "I can give . . . I can give you information. About The Syndicate. Whatever you want to know."

Not surprising, since the bastard wasn't loyal to anything. Still, he played along, humoring the man. "What can you tell me?"

"I can . . ." Hector thought for a second. "I can tell you that there's a change in leadership now. There were five before."

"I already know," the Shadow Man told him. "I killed three of them."

Hector gulped visibly. "And one of them killed the other. There's only one in power now."

Interesting. He must have missed that in the two months he'd spent with her, giving her all his time to heal slowly.

"What about the rest of the organization?" he asked, walking around in the shadows, watching the other men constantly turning to see where his voice was coming from.

"It's the same. They don't know about the change in leadership."

That meant Vin, Dante's man, didn't know about it either, which meant that entire side was still in the dark. Over the last few months, he had left breadcrumbs for them to find her, keeping them busy while buying himself more time, and mainly he had sent Vin chasing Lyla's friend, the girl who had been good to his little flame. For that alone, she deserved his consideration. While Vin had found a list of redheads in the business, Dainn had mainly had him focused on Malini, knowing that she would talk about her friend and give him a clue.

"And how do you know that?" he asked Hector. The man's brother, Victor, was rampaging through the underworld trying to find him, with no idea that he was in Gladestone. Too many people wanted a piece of Hector, and no one deserved it more than Lyla.

"This man . . . he was the one who contacted me when I worked for Alpha, about getting his sister-in-law," Hector elaborated. "Zenith was one of the girls who went missing twenty years ago. That was the last big batch they got, and it got fucked up because she had been the kid of some mafia boss."

Indeed she had been. Zenith had been the real Morana, which made him wonder about her.

"Why the attacks on Morana?" he asked, genuinely curious. That was the one thing he hadn't been able to put together.

Hector hesitated. "Her father had had information about The Syndicate. When they realized she was his child, they thought she had the information too, especially since she'd begun to dig into the organization. So they began to work to eliminate her."

Stupid of them, considering she had both Tristan's and Dante's protection. And unbeknownst to them, she had his protection too, mainly because of Xander. She was good for the boy, and he needed that. Until Lyla could decide for herself what she wanted to do with her past, he was going to keep an eye out for the kid, just like she'd asked him to. She could ask him to do anything and he would, and he wondered if she even realized half the power she had over him.

He circled around the small room again. "Tell me about this man, the leader."

Hector groaned, his arms shaking with his weight. He was hanging from the same chains he had put her in. "He's an older guy," the man began. "I haven't met him but his user account was 'thesyndicater03'. He was interested in Zenith. Wanted her bad."

"Why?"

"Because she escaped. She left behind L . . . Lyla."

He had not known that, but it made sense. Both girls had been taken together, so both girls had become friends. And Zenith had escaped as a child, leaving his little moon behind.

"Did the man punish Lyla for it?" he asked, wondering if he needed to add another reason to his list kill the man.

"I don't know. But he did keep her with him for a while before sending her out."

Hector was proving useful after all. Maybe he'd let him live another day.

He stepped behind the second man, the one who had been silent, the one who had also done lesser damage to her, and broke his neck in the blink of an eye.

Hector cried out in shock. "Please, no, I'll tell you everything else. Let me go."

The Shadow Man walked out, locking the room, as the cries followed. Mulling over the new information, he made his way back to the hotel, climbing the ladder and jumping into the room on quiet feet. His eyes went to her, to see her hogging his pillow and snoring softly, wrapped in the blanket like a burrito, and something inside his chest loosened at seeing her like that.

He headed to the bathroom to take a quick shower and wash the night off, before walking back to the room and rounding the bed to his side. He slowly slipped inside, adjusting her so as to not wake her, and she settled on him, clinging to his chest, her head on his arm, her lips parted, her eyes moving behind the closed lids as she dreamed of something.

Pressing a soft kiss to her delectable mouth, he hoped she dreamed of something nice as he watched her, marveling at the woman she had become. He had seen people through his life become monsters, especially people who had traumatic childhoods found it difficult to break the chains. And though he had helped her, she had been the one to always defy the chains, even bound to them. She had been the one to run off into the dark and save her child. She had been the one to endure punishment and keep her head high. She had been the one to live day after day just so she could know more about her son.

Pushing her flame hair back from her face, he wondered where she got the courage from, to keep going without letting the world tarnish who she was, without them extinguishing her light, without them taking away her ability to ceaselessly love. She faced her traumas with him and let him make another memory for it. She saw him for who he was and still looked at him with her heart in her eyes. She doubted herself everyday and still kept going on.

He didn't know if the tightness in his chest was what she called love, but he knew if there was an alternate reality where he could feel like normal people did, he would love her. His main motive now was to never let her long for that alternate version of himself.

CHAPTER 24

LYLA

Something was different.

Lyla didn't know what it was, or why she even felt something was changed. But the moment she woke up and started to leave the bed, iron bands wrapped around her middle tightened, holding her close.

"Dainn?" Her voice was soft, raspy from the sleep and his arms flexed against her stomach. She put her hands on them, scoring the muscular forearm with her nails, gently soothing whatever it was that was bothering him.

"I was nine the first time they came for me."

Her breath hitched. His past. He was thinking about his past, sharing it with her. *Finally.*

She began to turn but he held her in place, her back to his chest, his words moving over her head.

"By then," he continued quietly, "I already knew I wasn't like the other boys in the home. The Morning Star Home had so many of them, and I was like none of them."

The words penetrated her sleepy mind, clearing the fog. She looked at the open window, early morning light peeking from under the drapes, still leaving the room majorly in the darkness, right where he found comfort.

"What were you like?" she asked, her voice equally as low so as to not break the moment.

"Off." One word, a long pause. "I was off. I didn't feel what they felt, I didn't see things as they saw them, I didn't perceive the world as others did. My worldview even at a young age was skewed. I was selfish and easily angered, and if someone provoked me, I didn't feel any remorse in making them pay."

God, the way he spoke about himself as a child sent a tremor through her body. She tried to remember what she'd been like at that age—scared, lost, confused. She used to cry all the time, so much that the handlers had stopped punishing her for it because it only made her cry more. She'd felt too much, and it was such a contrast to who he had been.

Who he still was.

They were just both better at hiding it from the world.

She waited in silence, letting him continue at his own pace, not pushing him beyond whatever he was comfortable sharing.

"They came for me, when I was nine," he picked up from the previous thought. "Except they didn't know the kind of child I was. My eyes were always like this, and they called me 'demon child', thinking it would hurt me. I just smiled."

Damn. That made her hands falter for a second before they resumed stroking his forearms.

"I smiled as I ripped them away," he went on. Raising his hands slightly so see could see the burn scars on the back. "I didn't know how to play with fire back then and got these."

She traced the scars, not too prominent but present enough, and he turned his wrist, capturing her fingers, interlinking theirs together. "What happened then?"

He gave her hands a possessive squeeze before letting her hands go free, letting her stroke and soothe him again.

"I became a demon child in the true sense of the word," he proceeded, his words falling on her head. "I killed anyone who got near me without any remorse. The adults didn't know how to handle me. So, they brought in someone who wasn't like them."

Her breathing got heavier as she waited him out.

"A girl, a year younger than I was."

Fuck. Monsters. Every fucking one of them.

Her fingers tightened on his forearms but she remained silent, letting the rage infuse her body. She had lived enough in this world to know where this was going.

"She was a small thing, so helpless," he recalled. "I couldn't kill her. So they began using her as leverage to make me . . . do things."

She squeezed his arms, her body shaking, imagining the powerful boy he had been even as a child being controlled by those monsters, doing things he didn't want to because he didn't want to kill a helpless girl.

"What happened then?" Her voice broke, the tremor in her body audible in her tone.

"They used me for two years," he told her matter-of-factly, and she closed her eyes. *Not him. Not him too.* Yet, knowing he'd been through some of the same thing she had made her feel more seen, more connected to him. And knowing that, seeing how powerful he had become, it gave her hope for herself, that maybe she could break the shackles of her past and find power for herself too.

"She was the only girl living in the boys home, and only because they kept using her to control me. And she saw that. She knew I was a killer, and she kept begging me to kill her when the pain got too much. But I don't kill kids, not now, not back then."

She waited, her heart getting heavier with each word.

"So, one night when no one was watching, she killed herself."

Her breath hitched, her eyes squeezing shut, the pain for a soul lost heavy in the air. "What was her name?"

She felt his shrug. "I don't know. They called her 5057. I'm guessing wherever she'd been before didn't give the girls names like they did us."

That was sad, so fucking sad.

Engrossed in the tale, she moved, trying to turn around, and this time, he let her. She settled, fully facing him, seeing those mismatched eyes of his that had made him a demon child to the monsters. He was more. He was the devil and he was hers.

She placed her hand on his jaw, rubbing his scruff with her thumb, their eyes locked. "Then?"

"Then," he said, his voice a low rumble that rolled over her, his arms around her waist. "They let me go."

She blinked, surprised. "What?"

"They let me go," he repeated. "They knew with her gone they couldn't control me again, and I was already twelve, getting older, more dangerous. So they decided it was better to let me go than to keep me and risk everything."

She drew in a sharp breath. "Where did you go?"

"Nowhere, everywhere." His fingers traced her naked back under his t-shirt. "They left me on the streets, and I stayed there for some time, stealing what I had to. I squatted in a school for a while, pretending to be one of their students, using their resources. The school was some kind of specialized one, and they had a martial arts class they gave to kids after hours. That interested me, so I got in there too. Then I squatted in one of the empty houses in the rich neighborhood when the owners had been away somewhere."

That sounded wild to her, and absolutely terrifying. To be that young and be out in the world. "And nobody suspected anything?" she asked, both awed and scared at the thought that he'd lived through all that.

She saw his lips twitch, one of his hands coming to her jaw, thumb over her lips. "Just because I'm real with you doesn't mean I'm like this everyone, *little flamma,*" he told her almost affectionately. "I fool people. It's second nature to me. Even back then, I knew exactly what to fake into charming everyone into believing me, and they ate out of my hands. Boys wanted to befriend me, and I used them. Girls wanted to fuck me, and I used them."

Oh, the danger of him.

She wondered what it would have been like, in another reality, if she had been in that school with him. Would he even have taken a second look at her? Would he have manipulated her into believing he liked her when he just wanted something else all along? Was he manipulating her now?

The longer she looked at him, the more his lips curved in a smile, the tighter his grip got on her jaw. "Second thoughts?"

"If I had been a girl there," she worded her question but then left it, not wanting to know.

He rolled her under his body, his mouth inches from hers. "If you had been there, I would have fucked you. Then, I would have stalked you, and I would have made you mine. There is no reality where you and I exist that we don't end up exactly where we are now. None."

Inhaling deeply, she let her tight muscles relax as he kissed her, his tongue claiming her mouth, his hands claiming her body, his breaths claiming her heartbeats.

"What if I hadn't wanted to be yours?" she provoked him, because god she loved it when his eyes flashed the way they were.

"Let's not go there, Lyla."

The soft warning of his words did something to her. His nose brushed hers, his grip on her jaw firm.

She knew what he meant. He would've had her, by hook or by crook, with or without her initial consent to be his. For some twisted reason, the thought of that didn't fill her with dread as it should have. No. She had never felt more desired, more wanted, more powerful as she did when he told her this. And she didn't know if he said it just to manipulate her, or because he genuinely meant it, but given the last six years he had spent doing exactly that, there was little reason to doubt him.

He kissed her for a few minutes, as though cementing his words, before he lay back down on his side, this time staring up at the ceiling, one arm behind his head, the other around her. She snuggled into his side, waiting for him to pick the story back up again, enjoying the way his hand spanned her entire ass before his fingers began to stroke her spine.

"I never forgot what The Syndicate had done," he began again. "They made a massive mistake when they let me go. Exposing me to the outside world, it only made me realize how much power I had, and how much more I could have. Inside the home, I was limited about what I could do. Outside? The possibilities were endless."

They must have been for him. The dangerous boy he had been would grow up to be an even more dangerous man.

His voice didn't falter. "I didn't have any plans in the beginning. But I wanted to make them pay for what they'd done to me, and what they were doing to some of the kids in that house."

She was one hundred percent on-board with that. "What did you do?"

He slanted her a look. "I went back after a few years, once I knew they wouldn't be expecting me. Every year, all kids were taken to a different site for inspection while the adults stayed back."

"You went that day," she deciphered, knowing he would've wanted the kids to be out of his way. "What did you do?"

"I burned it all down," he stated. "Every inch of that ground, every brick of that house, I set it on fire. And I stood outside, enjoying the flames as they took everyone who had been inside. Alive."

She shuddered slightly at the vivid imagery she could see in her mind, yet no sympathy hit her for those who had burned away. They had deserved to burn in the hell they had created.

"That's when The Syndicate came to you?" She put the pieces together from what he'd told her. "And you worked for them for some time. But why go after them afterward, when you'd already destroyed those who'd hurt you? I don't understand."

He stayed silent for a long minute, simply staring up, his fingers lazily moving up and down her spine. She almost thought he wouldn't answer when he spoke up again.

"I began to collect information within the organization. I got to know about how many operations they had in how many locations, about the different trades they were in, about the powerful people on the outside who were involved in some way or the other. I took all the information, and I kept saving it. Knowledge is power after all."

Okay. That still didn't answer her question.

"It was in my last year working for them that I understood the structure of the organization. It's like a pyramid, with handlers at the bottom, their managers above them, then their bosses, and finally The Syndicate leaders themselves. None of the lower levels know anyone above beside their own contact. That's how the organization has worked for decades and kept everything secret."

Lyla stayed still, twining her legs with his to let him know she was there without breaking his flow.

"There are—or were—five leaders. The Syndicaters."

"Is that what they call themselves?"

A dark chuckle left him. "On the nose, isn't it?"

It was. But people like that with that high up the organization had to be full of hubris, so she wasn't surprised. "What do you mean there were five leaders?"

"Four of them are dead," he turned to look at her. "Now there's just one."

Her heart began to race at his words, at the implication. *No way.* She went up on her elbow, looking down at him in shock. "You mean if he is removed, the organization can . . . end?"

"It's more complicated than that," he explained, his eyes on her. "If he's removed, someone else would rise and fill the void. And organization such as this, that's existed for over five decades, it cannot be taken down in one strike."

"But you've been working on it for almost two of those decades, haven't you?"

"I have."

Why though? She didn't get that. It wasn't because of some kind of moral compass that he had—she knew his morality was as good as null when it came to anyone but her. Even the kids, he wasn't attached to but rather their helplessness made him step up. But a man like him, obsessed with taking the organization down, had to have some motive.

She didn't voice any of her thoughts, waiting patiently for him to elaborate.

His jaw worked.

"That last year I was there, amongst the data I had collected, I found my own file."

Oh.

Oh.

"I'd been bred to an underage girl by a man in his thirties," he stated matter-of-factly. "She killed herself after giving birth to me, and I was put into the home. My sire—"

She held her breath.

"—was a Syndicater at the time."

Speechless.

She was stunned *speechless.*

At her shocked silence, another dark chuckle left him. "I am the prince of this hell in every way. Fitting, isn't it?"

She couldn't say a word. She didn't know what word to say. So she lay her head on his chest, her heart thudding as his beat at a steady pace, pieces of this man falling into place.

CHAPTER 25

LYLA

The sun was setting in the sky as they walked down the city street. In her green sweater and navy jeans and white sneakers, her vivid read hair falling to the upper half of her back, she walked tucked under the arm of the most lethal man she knew. He was in his black jeans and a black sweater, his hands in the gloves he always wore on the outside, his face exposed to the cold wind.

And that in itself let her know exactly what they were going to do.

They said you only saw the Shadow Man's face right before you died, and with the exception of herself, she doubted it was false. And since they were going to see the bald man, she knew his time was up.

Still processing everything she'd learned about him that morning, Lyla took in the sight of the city as they moved by. Gladestone was surprisingly busy with people walking down the pavements, cars honking away in the traffic, street vendors selling things on the sides.

It was loud and populated and she didn't understand how a city like this had no idea of what went on within it. Or maybe it did. Maybe they all knew and nobody cared.

Dainn guided them to the left, into a narrower street that opened up into a quieter, more industrial area. There were still people milling about, workers going in and out of the factories, some of them stopping to give her a onceover before looking at the man at her side, and quickly looking away. That didn't surprise her one bit. Even without the shadows and the darkness, there was something inherently dangerous about him, something that warned the other person not to look too close before they couldn't look at all.

She tightened her arm around his waist, glancing up at him as they kept moving. "Why didn't we take the car?"

His eyes were vigilant even as he appeared casual, clocking everything and everyone. "It would've been too noticeable."

"And we aren't noticeable?" she laughed, shaking her head at the idea. He might not have been but she was attracting attention and they both knew it.

"Oh, but we're just two lovers out for a stroll," he informed her, his lips twitching.

She liked him like this. She didn't know if it was the fact that he'd shared so much of himself with her or that he was genuinely enjoying getting her vengeance or maybe both, but he felt lighter with her, and he was definitely more handsy than he had been. His hands had taken up residence on some part of her body or another all through the day and it felt newer, the way he touched her without sexual intent now. It felt . . . domestic almost, if they could ever be used with that word.

Taking a turn to the left, to a much more isolated part of the industrial area, Lyla looked around as any signs of inhabitation fell away.

"Why aren't there any people here?"

His eyes still sweeping the area, he answered. "Because this whole block is owned by a dead industrialist. His industries are collecting dust so to speak, and this area used to be the prime spot for his business. Now, lowlives use it sometimes."

He wasn't a lowlife, so she didn't understand why he was using it. But she kept the thought to herself as they headed to one of the factories right at the end of the walkway. The sun was almost close to setting, the sky a dark purple, and in the abandoned ghost block, she felt herself shudder. His arm tightened around her immediately, and the weight on her chest eased enough for her to breathe. No one would get to her, not with him right there.

She wanted to someday be able to protect herself, wanted to learn self-defense, but both Dainn and Dr. Manson were right about her needing more time.

'You have all the time in the world, Lyla. Heal yourself first.'

She needed to heal her mind enough not to freeze before she could fight, and she was a long way from that. But Dainn had promised her he would get her the perfect trainer who was her size when she was ready, and she trusted that. He had gotten her psychological help when she'd needed it without even knowing. He would get her physical help too when she was ready. She had asked why he wouldn't train her himself, since he was so well-versed in martial arts, and he'd just given her a heated look, letting her know exactly why for the next hour.

Shaking off her thoughts, she noticed the absence of wind right before they stepped into the old factory. Not knowing where they were going, she couldn't even see properly in the little light inside, but she followed his lead as he twisted and turned around the corners, finally coming to a stop in a really dark corridor.

He removed his arm from around her and turned to the side, holding her jaw in his hand, his mismatched eyes on her in the dark. "Be ready."

Taking a deep breath in, preparing her mind to see the monster who had broken her, she nodded.

Without a word, he opened a door she hadn't even seen, and entered. She turned her neck, taking a step across the threshold, and froze.

Her entire body locked in place. Not because of the man hanging from his arms. No. It was because of the room.

The room.

The same little bed in the corner.

The same dirty walls enclosing it.

The same cracked, dingy ceiling.

It was the room of her death.

And he'd brought her here.

Why?

She felt his lips at her ear, even though she couldn't see him in the little light.

"Feel it, *flamma,*" he whispered, his voice seductive in the face of her turmoil. "Feel everything you're feeling. Don't shove it under a rug, don't push it aside. What do you feel?"

Rage.

Pain.

Humiliation.

Fear.

So much.

"He's right there," the voice of death cajoled. "And he can't touch you. So feel, and do what you need to take back what he took from you."

She was feeling so much, her hands fisted at her sides, her body shaking with the force of everything hitting her. Her eyes swept the room, memories flooding her mind—of her on the bed, slowly dying, one shattered piece at a time, of her in the dingy bathroom, hacking off her hair, one lock at a time, of her sitting in the corner, arms around her knees, struggling to take one breath at a time. They had driven her to it, they had shoved her into the black hole she had resisted all her life, and fuck if it didn't make her fucking *angry*.

A noise she didn't even recognize left her chest, and the hanging man stirred.

Lyla trembled, rooted to the spot, watching as his head lolled and his eyes searched the room, stopping on one of his pals dead in a chair, before suddenly coming to where she stood.

The bald man grinned with a mouth full of blood. "A sight for sore eyes. Just the memory of your cunt gets me hard."

Disgust, so deep, rolled through her. She wished she'd lost her memory of everything, wished she couldn't remember what he was talking about, how her body had been degraded and her insides had screamed at him to get off her. But she remembered, every single thrust, every single time.

"You're going to die," she told him, her voice shaking with her rage.

The bald man swept his eyes around the room, unable to find the man he was afraid of. "So you're his whore now. I don't blame him. You did have the most amazing cunt to rape, and oh, I've been in many."

He was provoking her, and possibly also the Shadow Man he knew was around, she knew that. And yet his words kept hitting like bullets.

'Take back what he took from you.'

Power.

He had taken away her power, bleached it from her soul until she became a shell, and she was going to take it from him.

So, she took a step into the room, the stench making her want to gag. She took another deep breath, focusing on keeping her spine straight and not on the smell.

"You think you were a man?" she laughed, tilting her head to the side, imitating how she'd seen Dainn talking to other people when he had the upper hand. "Oh, my 'cunt' has been fucked and sorry to tell you, you didn't even scratch the surface." She examined him from head to toe, and shook her head. "Not even half the surface."

The ugly twist on his face told her she'd struck a nerve, and the rush of power it sent through her body made her heady. Keeping on, she dug deeper. "You worthless piece of shit, you couldn't even break a woman you held captive for months. You're not a man. You're a spineless swine masquerading as a man."

Oh that hit him. For whatever reason, he had a weak spot about his superior masculinity.

Lyla chuckled. "What? Mommy didn't love you as a boy? Did she tell you you were worthless too?"

"Shut up," he cut through, his voice enraged.

Lyla could feel the call of the cruelty, the power it held, so tempting. She could feel herself twisting and becoming something ugly to match him, to get one over him. But it wouldn't be her. She wasn't cruel, and the months she had spent healing and finding herself, she didn't know if going down this dark hole would undo them. Cruelty always cut the hand striking the blade.

It was too precious to risk.

But she wanted her vengeance. She wanted to see him hurt.

So far, the Shadow Man had been absent, letting her do whatever she wanted, giving her the freedom to take her power.

And she fucking loved him for it. She loved him for giving her a home, giving her a place to belong, giving her space to just be. And she loved him for bringing her to the place of her nightmares, for seeking vengeance on her behalf and stringing up the monsters, making her realize it all had no power over her anymore. She had grown, she had evolved, and the terrified, tired girl she had been didn't exist in this hellhole anymore. The woman she was now, the woman she wanted to be, didn't want to be cruel.

The smell of gasoline slowly filled the room.

Lyla looked around, trying to see where is was coming from, but couldn't see a thing.

So, she took a step back toward the threshold. "I feel pity for you," she told the bald man. "I feel pity that you never knew love. And I feel pity because you're going to die painfully all alone, knowing you were never loved."

His expression soured. "You think he loves you?" he spat out. "He's using you because of who you are, because of where you come from. Has he told you about it?"

She stayed still, her breaths locked in her chest.

The bald man laughed. "Has he told you about your brother? The man who's been looking for you for almost twenty years?"

Lyla froze.

What the fuck was he talking about?

He was lying. He had to be lying. She didn't have a brother. She had no family. No way.

Before the bald man could say another word, she felt the presence at her back.

"Trust me still?"

She closed her eyes at the words, the familiar words, and reminded herself that she'd trusted this man six years ago with her baby, and she trusted him now. She had been with him long enough to know he was motivated by her well-being.

"Yes," she whispered.

"Good girl." She felt a soft kiss to the side of her neck.

"Do . . . do I have a brother?" she asked, unable to help herself.

She felt a moment's pause. "Yes."

Her knees wobbled and she felt her body collapsing, his strong arm going around her waist to support her. "I was waiting for you to be ready. You couldn't have met anyone like you were."

She centered herself, holding onto his arm, her brain processing everything. She had a brother, one who'd been looking for her for twenty years or so, which meant he was older than she was.

She had an older brother.

She didn't know the emotions inside her, didn't know what was happening in her body as it sunk in. She was aware of the bald man saying something, and aware of the quiet but solid presence behind her, but nothing more.

She had an older brother.

Tears streamed down her cheeks, her nails digging into the forearms of the man she held onto, her breathing heavy. She trusted him, but she was *mad,* mad because he'd known about it and hadn't told her, mad because she had gone on for so long thinking she had no one. A part, one more rational, agreed with him, that she hadn't been ready mentally and emotionally for a news like that. But she was still *mad.*

She focused on the anger, routing it externally, and straightened from where she leaned against him.

Without a word, she felt him move away to the side. She watched as he picked up a canister and walked into the one ray of light coming in through the high window, his face exposed.

The bald man's eyes widened. "Blackthorne."

So, he recognized Dainn.

"I'll be damned," the bald man laughed, the sound hysterical. "Fucking Blackthorne."

Dainn didn't utter a word, simply opened the canister and tipped it to the side.

The pungent smell of gasoline filled the room as the liquid spread on the floor, Dainn stepping back casually from its range.

The bald man began to struggle. "Let me go. I will be useful to you, Blackthorne. I can help you get information. Please. Let me go."

The plea, so reminiscent of her own begging for mercy, left a sour taste in her mouth. She stayed in place as the gasoline spread on the floor right under him and his dead friend, watching Dainn stepping back until he was right at her side. Quietly, without taking his eyes away from the scene, he pulled her out of the room. Something cool, metallic found her palm.

Lyla looked down, seeing a lighter. *His lighter.*

He had given her his fire.

Emotions a flurry in her chest, she focused on the monster begging inside, channeling her fear and pain and rage to one source, and flicked the lighter open.

The sight of the flame had the bald man crying pitifully, and she felt the rush of power again. She'd never thought she would kill someone, but if there was one person who deserved to burn in hell, it was this man.

Without a twinge of doubt, remembering not only what he'd done to her but knowing what he'd done to so many others like her, she threw the lighter into the room.

As the flames began to spread, and screams rent the air, Lyla stood with her devil and watched one of her demons and one of her hells be destroyed.

CHAPTER 26

LYLA

The smell of burning flesh was putrid, almost enough to make her sick.

As the fire burned away at the room, the heat getting hotter on her skin, Lyla walked away from the corridor and out toward the exit of the factory, everything she was feeling, everything she had experienced and discovered crashing down on her.

She had a brother.

A few steps into the gloomy factory.

She had family.

Her breathing got choppy.

He hadn't told her.

Something tight invaded her gut.

Before she knew what she was doing, her feet were flying. She began to run, full-throttle, away from the fire, away from the hell, away from the man, nothing but rage pulsing in her head. She couldn't believe he hadn't told her, couldn't believe he'd not given her a single indication that he knew something about her past.

As her feet led her over the cemented floor right to the main entrance, she heard him call out for her.

"Lyla."

Just one word, and her feet faltered before she righted herself. "Do you know my real name?"

He paused, his eyes watchful. "Yes."

Fuck him.

She broke out into a full-speed run.

She needed to get away from him, needed to get some space before she did something she would regret, like scratch his mismatched eyes out.

The emotions swirling in a tornado inside her, she exited into the block, moonlight ample enough to show her the eerie quietness. She hesitated, wondering if she should go through the way they'd come, or take the left toward an unknown area. She looked back to check where he was, only to see him walking casually toward her, his hands in his pockets, eyes intent on her.

She hated that he was approaching her so slowly, that there was no urgency in his chase as there was in her heartbeats.

Fuck him. The thought was on repeat in her mind.

She pivoted left, and began to run to her full speed, her smaller frame quick, more agile, her eyes taking in the area. Industrial block after block passed, the space for her to run narrowing as the final block she crossed opened on some kind of dock but without any boats, just a stream of water spanning the vantage.

Turning, she began to run parallel to the river, not knowing where she was going, just knowing she needed to get away as the cemented path giving away to softer soil.

After a few minutes of running, with her lungs burning and her calves screaming, she stopped, resting her hands on her knees, catching her breath as she looked around for him.

She was alone.

Had he given up on chasing her? Or was he giving her space?

And she was messed up because she hated that. She'd expected him to be at the corner, expected him to be barreling down and taking her with him. She'd expected him to be there, but he wasn't, not as far as the eyes could see. She was in a strange place, all alone, and it was dark.

Tired, she walked to the wooden dock, right over the river, and slumped down on the slabs.

She sat there quietly, looking over the river and to the other side, the bank more forested than this side, and she began to shake.

She didn't know if it was the adrenaline from the running, or the high of the power, or the aftermath of her first murder, or the discovery of her long-lost family. She didn't know what it was, but as her tremors intensified and her eyes began to burn, she stared mindlessly at the water, her mind collapsing again into a kind of numbness that was terrifying her.

Arms came around her, a warm body at her back, legs on each side of her, his masculine scent in her nose.

"Xander is with your brother."

Five words.

Five words that tilted her world on its axis all over again.

She gripped his arms to anchor herself, her chest heaving as a noise left her, the burn overpowering her eyes. The shivers wracked her frame and she cried out, sobbing as the facts hit her one after the other.

She had a brother.

Her baby was with her brother.

She had family.

Her baby had family.

Her sobs turned to hiccups and she stared at the water, her throat burning.

"He's a smart kid," he told her, and she soaked his words, letting them water the waiting, parched parts of herself. "I hired an old woman to take care of him for the first few years while I tracked your history and where you'd come from."

"He . . . he knows you?" she stumbled over the question, unable to believe it.

His arms gave her a squeeze. "He does. I talked to him, explained that he had family he had to go to, and he understood. He's sharp. Then, I placed him in an orphanage and led your brother right to him."

She swallowed. "What's . . . my br . . . my brother like?"

There was a long pause. "He leads the mafia operations in Shadow Port. He's determined, lethal, and he's not stopped looking for you since you were taken from him twenty-two years ago."

The honest, matter-of-factness of his words made her close her eyes as she absorbed them. Her brother. He was in the underworld too. And he had been searching for her.

"What's his name?" her voice croaked.

"Tristan Caine," the man behind her spoke, his voice neutral.

"And . . . what's my name?"

A hand turned her face to the side, her eyes locking with his in the moonlight. "Luna."

Luna. It felt strange. She didn't feel like a Luna.

She looked at him, unable to process it all, unable to understand everything she was feeling. "Why didn't you tell me?"

He stayed quiet for a long minute, so long she almost thought he wouldn't answer her. "At first, I didn't know. By the time I did, you were starting to self-harm in thoughts, and I had to keep you hanging in for the answers."

"And you didn't think telling me I had a brother, that Xander was with family, would have helped me hang on?"

It was odd hearing the bitterness in her voice. He leveled a steady look at her. "Would it have? If I'd told you you had family and the kid was safe, would you have hung on?"

She didn't know. Back then, she'd been a different girl, with a mindset she didn't go into anymore. She didn't know how she would have behaved. But that didn't let his off the hook.

"And what about after? When you took me home? You still couldn't have said anything?"

He sighed, the only outward reaction to whatever was happening inside him. "You would have left me."

She blinked. "What?"

"If I'd told you then, you would have left me, and I didn't know if you'd return. And I couldn't risk that. Dr. Manson also advised me not to put too much on your mind."

She turned her neck away, unable to keep her eyes on him, anger coming to the forefront of her mind again. "So you lied to me by omission."

He didn't say anything.

A dark laugh left her. "So what? Now that I love you, it's okay for me to know? Was that your plan? To make my stupid heart fall for you every damn day until I had no choice but to be with you? So that even if I left, I'd be with you? Was that it?"

His silence spoke volumes.

Done with him, done with everything, she pushed off from the ground. He started to get up but she pushed her palm out, stopping him. "I can't see you right now. I need some fucking space. Don't you dare come after me."

His jaw clenched but he stayed where he was, and she walked away the same way she'd come, hands in her pockets, not looking back at him. She walked back to the industrial block, past the factory now burning, her eyes lingering on the flames and smoke of her past. Whoever she had been in there months ago, the shell of a girl, ashes of her own being, was gone. She had risen, been reborn, and watching the flames, she could feel the heat of their kiss on her skin. The fire, once terrifying, was now her lover, and it was this fire that had purified her, reset her, rekindled her.

Acknowledging that, remembering the power she had taken back before she had killed her tormentor, she walked past the factory and toward the main street, merging into the noise and hustle of the city. She didn't know if he followed her, and frankly, she didn't care. She just walked and walked and walked, one with the crowd, her mind numb and reeling simultaneously.

The scent of tea broke through her haze. She looked to the side to find a small food shop, the wonderful scent wafting from the inside, and she entered. It was quaint. Going to the back of the shop, she ordered herself some herbal tea and a pastry, and took her phone out. Dainn had given her the device when they'd left home, guiding her on how to use it for everything—from calling to paying someone to sending a text.

But as she stared at the screen, she opened the search bar, her fingers hesitating.

And then she typed.

'Tristan Caine'.

She found a few hits, some newspaper articles, some images. Hands shaking, she clicked on one of the photos, to look down at a good-looking man with bright blue eyes. Lyla stared at the photo for a long second, unable to grasp if it was his features that looked familiar or if she'd seen him somewhere. Scrolling to the next photo, she gasped. It was him with a brunette in glasses, both of them looking at each other, the caption reading *'Tristan Caine and Morana Vitalio rumored to be engaged'*.

Morana.

She remembered that name. She remembered the girl that night in her club, the night she had almost ended her life. He had been there. Her brother had been right there, and she hadn't even known. Instead, she had gone up to her room and overdosed herself.

The messed up situation messed with her head. She put the phone down, drawing in short, sharp breaths to calm herself.

Tristan and Morana were together, and they were taking care of Xander. That was good. That, at least, was the biggest relief she had felt in a long time. She didn't know what she was going to do, didn't know how she was going to process anything, but she was glad from the glimpse of them she'd had that they'd seemed good, good enough to raise her baby boy.

The waiter brought her tea and pastries, and she just looked at them blankly, unknowing about the outside world.

Her brother, Tristan, was looking for her, for the sister he'd lost. But she wasn't that girl anymore. She wasn't Luna, and she didn't know how she could meet him, didn't know how she could put her broken self out there. What if she didn't live up to who he had in his mind? What if she wasn't enough? What if she fell short? Would he be disappointed that he'd spent so much time looking for her? Would he be frustrated and try to make her into someone else? And after all this time, would she be able to trust anyone on the outside? What did she even know about family? And what about Xander? What would she even say to him? If he was happy and settled, how could she ever destroy that?

As the self-sabotaging thoughts filled her mind, she closed her eyes and snapped the hair tie on her wrist.

It didn't work.

Thoughts and questions swirled in her head, drowning her, and she breathed through her mouth, trying to calm herself down.

It didn't work.

The phone in her hand vibrated, an unknown number calling. Focusing on her breathing, she picked up, staying silent.

There was silence on the other end.

She looked down to see if the call was still engaged, and put it back to her ear. There was a dark chuckle on the other end. Slightly creeped out, she bit her lip.

"Luna Caine," a man's deep voice, evil voice said over the line. "The bane of my existence for twenty years."

She gripped the phone in hand. "You've got the wrong number."

"No, little girl," the familiar voice spoke. "I've got the right number. Do you remember me?"

Her heart began to pound, old, old memories washing over her mind.

'Such a pretty little girl.'

She began to shake.

"I'm going to kill your lover, sweetheart," the evil voice told her. "The Shadow Man will die. Your brother will die. I've let you all live for too long. And then, when he is finished, I will take you for myself just like I did when you were younger. Do you remember?"

Bile rose in her stomach, climbing her throat. She swallowed it down, reminding herself she wasn't that scared little girl anymore, tat she was a grown woman, one who had just murdered one of her demons.

"Wrong number," she said, before hanging up the phone. She looked around the little place, noticing some people looking her way but unable to discern if it was dangerous. There were too many people.

She needed to get out.

Paying for the untouched order, she ran outside the shop and hailed a cab, giving him the name of the hotel.

As the city flew by, she closed her eyes, giving herself a moment of respite before everything crashed around her again.

CHAPTER 27

LYLA

He was waiting for her when she entered the room, his elbows on his knees, his eyes on the door.

Looking at him, after the space she'd taken, everything she'd been holding together crumbled.

He was up and around her before she could blink, his arms holding her tight, his chest against her face, and she breathed him in, shaking, shivering, sobbing.

"I'm so mad at you," she told him between hiccups.

"I know, *flamma*," he spoke quietly, his words against her hair. "I know."

"And I'm mad that your plan worked," she grumbled into his chest.

He pressed a soft kiss to her head, before pulling back, pressing an even softer one to her lips. "I don't regret doing what I had to do for us to be here."

"Do you regret anything at all?" she asked him, their eyes locking together.

"I regret that you were hurt."

That was all. But she didn't know why she was surprised. She knew who he was, how he operated, how his system worked. Somehow, in the midst of his extreme and her extreme, they'd struck a balance—where he took from her what she gave and she took from him what he gave. She couldn't forget that. But she was still mad, and she needed him to be mad, to work this anger out of herself in some way.

She pushed him away, going to the shower, and was aware of him following her, his eyes curious on her changing expressions. "I'm feeling too much right now," she told him, stripping her clothes. "So much I feel like I'm going to explode without figuring a thing out."

He tilted his head to a side. "What are you feeling?"

She locked their eyes in the mirror's reflection, provoking him. "Imagine that I'm leaving you." She saw his body stiffen. "Imagine that this is the last time you'll touch me." His eyes blazed. "Imagine that you can't do anything to stop it. Think of that, and how pissed you'd be. Would you even be angry?"

"I don't know if it'll be anger," he stated softly. "But if that ever happened, there would be absolute annihilation."

She shivered, her hands gripping the counter. She needed something, something to calm the tornado inside her, she didn't know what, and she looked at him, begging him to understand and give it to her.

He came to stand behind her, his eyes steady on hers. "Trust me still?"

With everything she was feeling, everything that had unraveled over the last few hours, she looked at him. Stupid fucking heart, still trusted him.

Taking her silence for the answer it was, he took a step closer, coming to loom over her. "Trust me still?"

The question, asked again, only told her that he wanted her answer verbalized.

"Yes," she told him. She did. Despite everything, she did.

A soft kiss pressed to her head. "Good girl."

Before she could say another word, she was bent over the counter, her breasts pushed against the sink, her ass out as he held her down with one hand on the back of her neck.

His other hand rubbed her ass cheek softly, the callouses on his hand stroking against soft skin, before he smacked it.

She yelped, her heart pounding as she looked straight into the mirror, her eyes locking with his.

"You will release everything inside you, *flamma,*" he commanded her, his voice low. "Every time my hand comes down, you will release whatever you're holding onto, and you will give it to me. Understand?"

Her chin began to quiver. "Yes."

Eyes locked with hers, his palm came down on her other cheek, harder than the first. She exhaled deeply and closed her eyes, imagining herself letting go. She could let go. She could be free. She knew it because she'd had it, and she could have it again. The past didn't have any control over her anymore.

His hand came down again, and a cry left her unbidden. "I hate you for keeping the truth from me."

He rubbed her rump, before smacking her, right above her thigh. That stung, but it felt so good. "I don't think my brother will want me after he gets to know me. There's . . . no way."

As the words left her, she began to cry.

He didn't say anything, letting her put it all out. When she quietened a bit, he spanked her again, stirring another well inside her.

"I don't want to go back into Xander's life and destroy him."

And so it went.

Over and over, until every single secret and every single thought she held onto was out, the weight of the burden blank from her mind, her sobbing as she broke down. After countless spanks, until her ass was on fire and her mind at rest, she felt him pick her up gently and carry her to the bedroom, holding her close as she cried into his neck, letting out everything, releasing everything, letting go of everything that was holding her down, at least for a while.

Crying, in his arms, she passed out.

She stirred awake to see him sitting with his laptop on the desk, looking at the screen in the darkness of the room, his face lit up by the glow from the monitor.

Turning, she wrapped the sheet around herself and padded over to him.

"Come here," he spoke, opening his arms and letting her sit on his lap, caging her in as he turned her back to the screen, and kept working through some numbers.

She blinked, not understanding what she was looking at, but she let him work through it, semi-napping on him.

"Remember when I told you about my friend who ran away?" she asked him, feeling him still beneath her at the question.

"Yes," he waited for her to continue.

She stared at the screen, remembering mindlessly. "The man she escaped from, he kept me with him for a few years. He ... he was the first."

He was still, utterly still, but remained silent.

"He called me tonight."

His hands were turning her around on his lap before she could blink, his devilish mismatched eyes intense on her. "Who?"

She shook her head. "I don't know his name. But he said . . . he threatened to kill you, to kill my brother. He . . . said he wanted to keep me again." Her voice trembled on the last words, and his grip on her jaw tightened.

"Not happening."

Two words, spoken with such ferocity she felt it seep into her bones.

"He's in The Syndicate?"

She nodded. "I think so. He addressed me by my real name."

He gazed at her for a long second. "Then you will have him at your mercy."

She never, ever wanted to see him again.

Dainn pressed a kiss to her neck, turning her around to face the monitor. "Full disclosure—I found your friend who ran away."

Lyla watched as he opened a folder, clicking on a photo. It blew up to show a beautiful girl, her eyes shining with happiness as she grinned at the camera. Lyla blinked, touching her hand to the face on the screen, remembering the girl who had left her behind. But she was happy.

"Where is she?" her voice cracked, her heart full for the little girl who had found a good life for herself.

A long pause in his reply made her turn her neck.

"She died. The bald man killed her."

Her hand dropped from the screen, her shoulders slumping. For the first time since the fire, she felt glad that he was already dead, because the coil of fury inside her made her want to murder him again. *Fuck.*

"She was adopted by a family, but originally she had been the daughter of the Shadow Port mafia boss." The information rolled over her as he brought up an image of Morana, the girl with the glasses. "Morana Vitalio was replaced by her."

Another photo came on, this one with Morana and a man holding her.

"That's your brother, Tristan," he told her, letting her soak their images.

"I saw them that night, you know," she whispered, her eyes scanning as another photo took its place. "The night I tried to . . ."

"I know. They were there that night following a lead. That's what I tapped into."

The photo changed, this time to include a young boy with the couple.

Her mouth parted, her eyes misting as she took in every single detail of his grown-up face. He was beautiful. So beautiful.

She wrapped her arms around herself as the photos changed, a slideshow of different shots of him, and Lyla took them all in, saving the precious visuals in her memory, her heart bursting with love and loss and happiness for him.

She burrowed into the solid body at her back, breathing though her mouth to control the flood of emotions inside her. He didn't know what he had given her, didn't know what he had done for her, for six years, day after day, night after night. For a man who said he didn't feel, he had raised a boy and sent him to his family, looked over him from afar while keeping her safe throughout. He had stayed with her when she'd been broken and given her all the tools she needed to gather the pieces. He had glued the pieces together and kissed her scars, making her belong in a way her heart had hungered for so deeply.

For a man who said he didn't feel, he sure loved her a fucking lot.

She turned her face to him, her heart in her eyes. "Thank you."

He said nothing, just held her, his eyes searching hers.

She pressed her lips to his and he took over, kissing her in the way she loved, in the way of claiming and owning and keeping.

And sitting in the arms of the devil she loved, not knowing what the future held for her, she felt hope. She felt safety. She felt love.

Whatever the future held, with him at her side, she would be okay.

They would be okay.

HIM

The shadow man looked down at the woman sleeping on the bed.

A girl who had crashed into his life, a light glow in the dark, thrusting life into his cold, dead heart.

Now a woman who had beaten odds, every single day, and come out rising on the other side, with so much life inside her he wondered how a single being could contain it. It had been that life that had hooked him, the vitality that fed into his void, the absolute to his abyss.

She had told him oncc, a checklist of all that love was to her, and she had fit every single category for him, all except one.

He had never, not once, put the good of anyone else before his own selfish needs, had never thought he would. But oddly, as he watched her sleep, knowing the demons she fought and the cracks she counted within herself, he felt a compulsion to cover the cracks and seal them shut, until she was back on the road to her healing as she had been.

He had seen how well she did when she focused on herself, when outside forces weren't pulling away at her, and he wanted her to find her way back to it.

And he knew what she needed to heal did not align with what he wanted, which was to keep her to himself and not share even a part of her with the world.

He traced her mouth with his thumb, and her lips parted in her sleep.

He wondered if there would ever be an end to this obsession, to this deep, dark need that breathed inside him with her heartbeats. For six years, it had only grown bigger, until it had consumed every single part of him, and he wondered if there was more of him left to consume. It was a marvel, how this tiny girl who had never been on anyone's radar had found herself embraced in the arms of death.

Taking a breath, an odd tightness in his chest, he opened his tablet and the thread of texts he'd sent Morana through changing IP addresses, dropping yet another morsel, a big one, for her to dig. Given her skills, she would probably crack it in two days, trace the file he had waiting for her, and get in touch.

For two more days, he would have his *flamma* just to himself, before her past came knocking, her brother finally finding her. He hated Tristan Caine just for that. But he would tolerate him, let him have his space in her life, if only for her. Because it would make her whole, make her heal, knowing that love too.

"Dainn?"

The soft, cracking voice brought his eyes back to the only being who mattered to him, the sweet aftertaste of her voice on his tongue.

"Come to bed," she grumbled, still half-asleep, and fuck if the tightness in his chest didn't intensify. He had once stood on cold streets, searching for warmth until the frost froze his heart. Even after he built himself the warmest of houses, the cold never left. Not until her, not until the only person who cared for him, cared that he wasn't sleeping, cared that he wasn't warm.

Following her soft request, he climbed back to his side, and felt her wrap herself around him, no hesitation in the way she clung to his body, pressed herself into his side, her face in the crook of his neck. She touched him like he wasn't an abhorrence to humanity, like he mattered, she always had. It had surprised him at first, the way she freely gave her touches to him, and he hadn't known how to react, not until he had begun listening to some deep-rooted instinct that knew exactly how to respond to this woman.

Listening to the same instinct, he wrapped his arm around her, holding her close.

"Dainn?"

Fuck, her voice still made his body vibrate with sensations.

"I love you."

He closed his eyes for a split second at those words, the tightness in his chest moving, roiling, until it was weighing him so heavy he couldn't breathe. Just for a split second, before he turned, gazing down at the woman he would wreck everything for, seeing her soft face and beautiful smile and sleepy eyes.

He wasn't a believer, but she was his miracle.

He didn't know if what happened inside him where she was concerned was love. It felt wrong to say that. Love was light, love was beautiful, love was pure. What he felt was dark, obsessive, deviant, and utterly possessive. He would kill for her, as he always had, and he would die for her, if need be. He would slay her demons and give her the sword to slay them if she wanted. He would hold her close and protect her from anything wanting to tarnish her being.

She completed parts of him that had been jagged and raw, fitting inside them with softness and fluidity, soothing some latent beast within him.

Where she loved him with all her light, he possessed her with all his shadows.

That's why she was his.

As he braced himself for the two days he had before their world changed, he held her, knowing that despite whatever came their way, he was never, ever letting her go.

And if anyone tried . . . *it would be the end.*

The Dark Verse series ends with Book 6, The Syndicater, coming later in 2022.

It will be a multi-POV novel featuring all the couples, wrapping up the final threads of the plot, leaving a fitting finale for the series, and epilogues for all the couples. It will be a live release.

To make sure you don't miss the notification, subscribe to RuNyx's Newsletter.

Thank you for reading. If you've enjoyed this book, please take a second to leave a rating/review.

ACKNOWLEDGMENTS

This book was the heaviest for me to write, both because of the subject matters and because of my own mental health when I wrote it and the issues I had while releasing this. As we get closer to the end of the series, it's even more bittersweet for me because this world has been my home for over six years.

It was tough and I need to thank a few people for making this book and my writing journey what it is.

To my readers, the ones who've been with me since the beginning, you're my OGs. It's incredible how you've been on the ride with this series even after so long. To my new readers who've just hopped on, your excitement is infectious! Thank you for giving me such joy and strength to persevere, especially with this series. This will always have the most special place in my heart.

Second, to my parents—I don't think I'd be here if it wasn't for you. Thank you for loving me so unconditionally and reminding me of it when I need regardless of the distance between us. I'm so lucky to be yours. I love you.

To the book community that has showered me with such love and kindness. To all the bloggers and bookstragrammers and booktokers, artists, editors, photographers, reviewers, friends I've made, thank you. Your love and your generosity means the world to me. Thank you so much for everything!

To my Firebirds and Ravens and Minions—thank you for being in my little bubble in my corner of the internet. You're the most amazing group of people.

And to Nelly. You're my hero. There will never be enough words in my heart to thank you for everything. You give the perfect visual to my words, somehow taking what I have in mind and making it a gazillion times better. Thank you!

To Emily, for being a rockstar of a PA and keeping everything organized for me because we both know I'm shit at remembering stuff.

To Valentine PR for being so incredible with this mess of a release. Thank you!

To my friends, for loving me when I fall off the face of the earth for days and come back like I never left, thank you for putting up with me.

All of you make my world a better place.

Most importantly, I want to thank ***you,*** the one reading this, for picking up my book and choosing to read me. If you've made it this far, I'm eternally grateful to you. I hope you enjoyed it but even if you didn't, thank you for choosing it. I appreciate you taking the time so much. Please consider leaving a review before jumping into your next bookish world.

Thank you so much!

CONNECT WITH RUNYX

Newsletter: https://runyx.kit.com/newsletter

Reader Group: https://www.facebook.com/groups/runyx/

Facebook: https://www.facebook.com/authorrunyx

Instagram: https://www.instagram.com/authorrunyx/

Website: https://runyxwrites.com/

Turn the page for an exclusive extract of ENIGMA . . .

DEATH SMILES . . .

Unknown Girl, Mortimer University

The girl stood on the edge of the cliff.

There was no moonlight for anyone to witness her demise, not a concerned soul around to make her question herself, not a sound beyond the sea and the whispers of her own moral decay.

Oh, she was of sound mind and judgment. Yet, she stood on the cliff on that moonless night, walking to her own destruction, an invisible gun of her own making to her head.

Maybe, things would have been different, could have been different, if she just had the courage. The world thought she was brave. They would remember her as such. There was nothing to indicate otherwise. Would this be a murder or a suicide or an accident? Would she become the girl on the news pushed by invisible hands, or a girl who jumped of her own free will? Or maybe, they would speculate a tragic fall of a girl who wandered too close to the edge. Literally, metaphorically, who knew?

The wind whistled around her, blowing her dress up and whipping her hair over her face. To anyone watching, she would have painted an ethereal, haunting picture.

Picture. Photographs. Memories.

She had so many of them.

She didn't want to stand on that cliff.

But she had to. There was no other choice, not for her.

Not when they were watching.

And they were always watching.

Even as she stood weighing her decision, her choices, her mortality.

Even as she stepped closer to the edge, her body shaking, resisting the directives of her mind.

Even as she closed her eyes and took the plunge, the wind rushing in her ears, the silence shattered by her scream piercing for a split second before cutting off abruptly.

They were watching as she lay on the dark sand on a dark night, and died.

The thrilling dark academia college romance.

DISCOVER THE MOST LOVED MAFIA ROMANCE SERIES

On a station platform, with nothing to read,
and a four-hour train journey stretching ahead of him...

That's where the story began for Penguin founder Allen Lane. With only 'shabby reprints of shoddy novels' on offer, he resolved to make better books for readers everywhere.

By the time his train pulled into London, the idea was formed. He would bring the best writing, in stylish and affordable formats, to everyone. His books would be sold in bookstores, stationers and tobacconists, for no more than the price of a ten-pack of cigarettes.

And on every book would be a Penguin, a bird with a certain 'dignified flippancy', and a friendly invitation to anyone who wished to spend their time reading.

In 1935, the first ten Penguin paperbacks were published. Just a year later, three million Penguins had made their way onto our shelves.

Reading was changed forever.

—

A lot has changed since 1935, including Penguin, but in the most important ways we're still the same. We still believe that books and reading are for everyone. And we still believe that whether you're seeking an afternoon's escape, a vigorous debate or a soothing bedtime story, all possibilities open with a book.

Whoever you are, whatever you're looking for,
you can find it with Penguin.